W0027720

tive to do nothing until a fuller conference later that day.

At 9 a.m. the distraught father received a letter marked 'special'. The message was typewritten on two pieces of paper. It began, 'Dear Sir', and told Jacob Franks that his son would be released in exchange for a ransom of $10,000. This was to be composed of old bills – the letter gave precise instructions about the denominations – which were to be placed inside a cigar box, or cardboard box, wrapped in paper and sealed with wax. Mr Franks was to have the package ready by 1 p.m. and then to sit by the telephone. He was forbidden to contact the police.

Ransom threat

The letter promised that Bobby Franks would be returned safe and well within six hours of the ransom being paid. 'Should you, however, disobey any of our instructions, even slightly, his death will be the penalty,' it warned.

Mr Franks went to his bank to withdraw $10,000 made up of $8,000 in $50 bills, and $2,000 in $20 dollar bills, as laid down by the kidnappers.

At noon the police informed him that the body of a young boy had been found by a railway worker wedged in a concrete drainpipe on a remote bank of Wolf Lake by the railway track. At 3 p.m. the telephone rang again. It was the kidnapper 'Johnson', telling him that a taxi would shortly arrive to take him to a drugstore. The taxi came but, as Franks was about to leave with the ransom money, the telephone rang again. It was his brother-in-law, Edwin Gresham. He had identified the body in the drainpipe as that of young Bobby.

The most intensive manhunt in Chicago's history was launched. The newspapers became almost hysterical, and the police subjected teachers from the young boy's school to harsh interrogation in the hope of proving that one of them was responsible. The taxi-driver sent to collect Jacob Franks was cleared. He had simply been hired by

Chicago was a rough city, but the killing of Bobby Franks shook the population. Police and rail workers (left) stand sadly by the culvert (below) where his body was found near Wolf Lake.

Hulton-Deutsch Collection

FAST-TALKER

THE VICTIM

AP/Wide World

Bobby Franks was the third child born to Jacob and Flora Franks, a Jewish couple whose families had settled in Chicago in the 19th century. However, Bobby had followed his parents into the Christian Science faith. Although they lived amongst the rich leaders of Chicago's Jewish community, the Franks had never been accepted socially.

At the local Harvard School, Franks was considered a brilliant student, with a flair for debate. Two weeks before his death, the 14 year-old had taken part in a school debate on capital punishment, arguing for its abolition. He also loved baseball and tennis, and was a lively, smiling, fast-talking youth who – superficially – resembled Richard Loeb himself.

telephone and went to the address as instructed. One man revealed that he had retrieved a blood-stained taped chisel which he had seen thrown from the car.

The typewriter – an Underwood – which had been used to prepare the ransom note was recovered from the bottom of a lagoon in Jackson Park. At the same time, an enthusiastic 18

We just decided to pick the most likely-looking subject that came our way

NATHAN LEOPOLD

year-old student named Richard Loeb, a fan of detective fiction who kept newspaper accounts of the Franks killing, volunteered to help three newspaper reporters who were covering the case. Loeb told the reporters that the kidnappers' call was probably made from a drugstore on 63rd Street and escorted them through the drugstore in the hope of tracking down the kidnappers.

New York Daily News

Sven Englund (above), the Leopold's chauffeur, shattered the killers' alibi. Loeb saw that resistance was futile. 'I'll tell you the entire truth . . .' he told the investigators.

BREAKTHROUGH

EVIDENCE?

It seemed at first that the spectacles (below) found near the body of Bobby Franks would be unlikely to provide a clue as to the identity of the murderer. They were very ordinary and the prescription for the lenses was extremely common. There were thousands of pairs like them in Chicago. But the hinge on the glasses was a patented article, manufactured by only one company in Chicago, Almer Coe and Company.

Furthermore, Almer Coe had been handling this frame and hinge for just a few months and only three pairs containing that fitting had been sold. One was to a lawyer, who had been in Europe for the last six weeks and another to a lady who still wore them. The third was supplied to a young man called Nathan Leopold Jr. He lived at 4754 Greenwood Avenue, very close to the Harvard School for Boys.

UPI/Bettmann Newsphotos

Then came a more significant clue. A railway signalman, working near the spot where the body had been found, had discovered a pair of horn-rimmed spectacles, which were traced to a young man called Nathan Leopold Jr.

Nathan Leopold was 19 years old, the son of one of the best known millionaires in Chicago. Known as 'Babe' because he was the youngest of six children, Leopold was extraordinarily intelligent. He had already been awarded a Bachelor of Philosophy degree from the University of Chicago, and was currently studying law at the Chicago Law School. He was regarded by his contemporaries as something of a genius, for whom no subject was too complex, nor any reading too tedious.

By the age of 18, he had taught himself nine foreign languages, and was an accomplished botanist. He had also made a special study of the German philosopher Friedrich Nietzsche. With money, brains and status, Nathan seemed destined for a glamorous career, probably in public life – until the horn-rimmed glasses left near Bobby's body were found to be his.

Leopold did not deny ownership. When he was picked up on 29 May by two detectives and taken to be questioned by the State's Attorney, Robert Crowe, at the La Salle Hotel, he was self-assured and unperturbed. Yes, he had a pair of horn-rimmed glasses, but he wore them only for bird-watching and had not used them lately. They were probably in an old suit at home which he kept for his bird-watching outings.

Flawed alibi

The detectives drove Leopold home again to look for them. They could not be found. Leopold remained calm. The railway bank where Bobby Franks' body had been discovered was a well-known haunt of bird-watchers and Leopold had often been there. He taught ornithology and had taken his class there more than once. The glasses had probably fallen out of his pocket on one such occasion weeks before.

The detectives persisted. Which pocket did he keep them in? The breast pocket. How would they have fallen out? He said he must have tripped. They asked him to show them exactly how. Leopold repeatedly tripped on the floor in front of the lawyers and detectives, but the glasses, placed by him in his breast pocket, stubbornly refused to be dislodged. Again and again he tried, succeeding only in making himself look foolish. For the first time, the detectives began to suspect that perhaps this golden boy could indeed be the killer of Bobby Franks.

Under pressure

They intensifed the questioning, going over the same points remorselessly for hours on end. The suspect grew restive. How could they suspect him? Bobby Franks was a nice little boy, Leopold said. The idea of ransom was absurd. He could have whatever money he wanted, whenever he wanted, simply by asking his father. Besides,

THE PARTNERSHIP

BACKGROUND

The criminal partnership of Loeb and Leopold had begun in 1921, three years before the murder of Bobby Franks. It began with petty thefts from a shop and hotel before the pair began stealing cars. On one occasion, chased by a truck, they jumped out of a car they had just stolen, leaving the vehicle to crash while they escaped. Leopold took part when he thought the thrill warranted the danger. Twice they were shot at while making their getaway.

Loeb enjoyed telephone crimes. Alone, he made obscene calls to people he disliked and, with Leopold, reported imaginary fires, enjoying the mayhem this caused. Loeb even became annoyed or disappointed if his petty crimes went unreported in the newspapers.

They soon began real fires, getting a kick out of being the only people who knew how the fires were started. Tiring of this, Leopold and Loeb turned to burglary. In November 1923, they stole the portable Underwood typewriter from student rooms at the University of Michigan. On this raid, Loeb carried a gun.

Jacob Franks, the victim's father (left), seen with his elder son Jack Franks, was fully convinced by the ransom note (below) that the kidnappers were capable of murdering his son. Franks soon learnt that the threat had already been carried out.

Left: Hulton Deutsch Collection; right: UPI/Bettmann Newsphotos

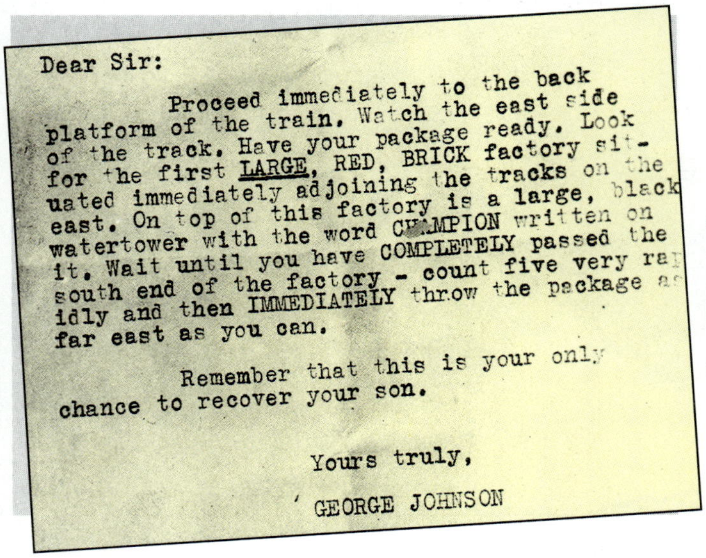

Dear Sir:

Proceed immediately to the back platform of the train. Watch the east side of the track. Have your package ready. Look for the first LARGE, RED, BRICK factory situated immediately adjoining the tracks on the east. On top of this factory is a large, black watertower with the word CHAMPION written on it. Wait until you have COMPLETELY passed the south end of the factory - count five very rapidly and then IMMEDIATELY throw the package as far east as you can.

Remember that this is your only chance to recover your son.

Yours truly,

GEORGE JOHNSON

he was paid for giving lessons in ornithology. And he did not own an Underwood typewriter.

Attorney Crowe and his assistants then asked Leopold where he was on 21 May. Over a week had passed but the young man seemed to remember precisely. It was the day he had taken his car out of the garage and gone with a friend to pick up two girls at Lincoln Park. After further questioning, Leopold reluctantly gave the name of his companion, an 18 year-old named Richard Loeb. Leopold said he had not mentioned Loeb before because the girls they had been with were not very respectable.

> **I can recall no feeling then of remorse. Remorse did not come until later, much later**
> NATHAN LEOPOLD

AP/Wide World

Their jauntiness fast disappearing, Leopold (left) and Loeb are led into Cook County jail after their arrest.

Richard Loeb was also rich and also a brilliant scholar. His father was the retired vice-president of the huge mail-order business, Sears, Roebuck and Co, and young Loeb was the youngest ever graduate of the University of Michigan. He had $3,000 in his bank account, and his father's secretary had instructions to make out cheques for him at any time.

The Leopolds' chauffeur, Sven, was called in. He had been with the family for nearly 19 years, since Nathan Leopold was a few months old. He said there was one day the previous week that Nathan had not taken his car out of the garage. He remembered it precisely because it was the day his wife, Alma, had gone to the doctor.

Leopold's alibi was destroyed. He had not been in his car with Richard Loeb in Lincoln Park – in fact he had not been in his car at all, for it had remained in the garage.

By this point Attorney Crowe was past being patient and polite. He told Leopold bluntly that his men were at a police station seven miles away taking a full statement of confession from Richard Loeb, who had been taken in for questioning the day before, 30 May. Crowe no longer needed Leopold to tell the truth – he already had it. Following the relentless questioning, this news drained Leopold of all resolve. He confessed that he and Loeb had killed Bobby Franks, though Loeb had struck the blow.

UPI/Bettmann Newsphotos

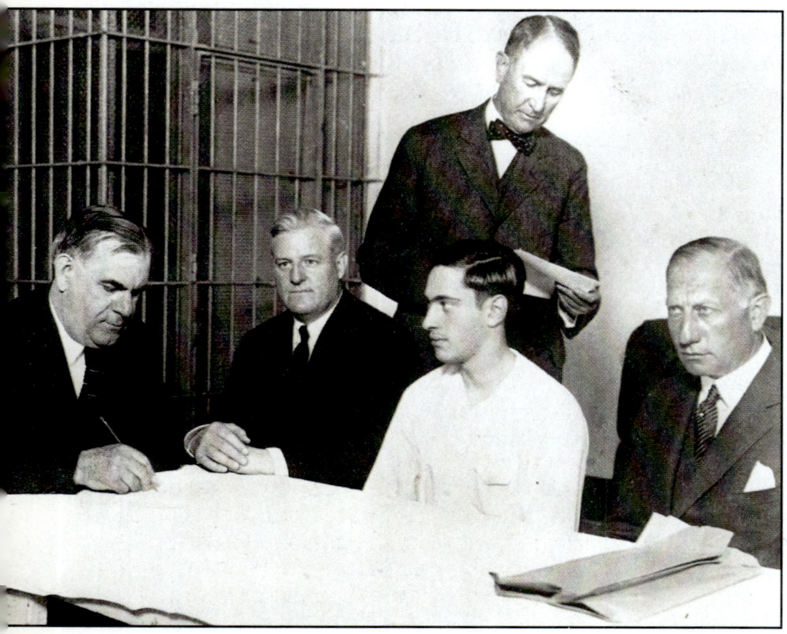

The baffling task of probing the motives behind the murder was begun by a succession of psychiatrists. Leopold (left, centre) relished the chance to talk about himself. He is seen with (left to right) Dr James Whitney Hall, Dr William Hickson, Dr Sanger Brown and a defence attorney, Ben Bachrach.

Coming clean

The two boys were brought together before a panel of psychiatrists and made to tell their stories in each other's presence. Leopold was given pen and paper so he could make notes if Loeb got something wrong. The notes were later handed over to Attorney Crowe, who thereby had written as well as oral confessions to the crime. The stories told by these two smart, clever, sophisticated boys revealed an account of a killing so pointless as to be without parallel in the history of murder.

EARLY DAYS

BAD DREAMERS

Leopold and Loeb never grew up. They had children's dreams and believed in them. But where their cruelty came from remains a mystery.

Both Nathan Leopold and Richard Loeb had enjoyed lives of extreme privilege. Their families had large and beautiful houses in Kenwood, the smartest and most exclusive suburb of Chicago, and they had been to the best schools.

Both boys had been raised by nurses and governesses in households filled with servants, both had unlimited pocket money and bank accounts with balances in excess of many working men in the 1920s. They drove their own cars long before car ownership had become commonplace. They had long expensive holidays in Europe and elsewhere.

They had everything money could buy and they were hopelessly spoilt by their families, in awe at their intelligence. There was little doubt that, but for the murder of Bobby Franks, they were each destined for careers which would take them to the very top of American society.

Sickly child

Nathan Leopold was born in Chicago on 19 November 1904, the youngest of three sons of Nathan Sr and Florence Leopold. The family were respected members of the Jewish community in Chicago, and among the wealthiest. Nathan Sr made his money in the shipping and paper industries.

'Babe' Leopold was precocious but was a child of poor health. Until the age of nine, he suffered from gastro-intestinal complaints, which were further complicated by fever, headaches and bouts of vomit-

Under the influence of his governess, Loeb was an unnaturally studious child. Here, he is seen at work on the journal he started, at a young age which he called 'Richard's Magazine'.

UPI/Bettmann Newsphotos

BIRD MAN

Nathan Leopold was among the most ardent young ornithologists in the US. Despite his insatiable appetite for reading and studying, he spent many hours each week touring the woods and marshes around his home city, studying bird-life. In the spacious third-floor study of the Leopold family mansion, he kept 3,000 specimens of birds.

His knowledge and dedication to the subject were enough to secure him a permit from the municipal authorities to shoot birds, with any of several privately owned guns, in public parks. Leopold also took regular groups of less experienced bird-watchers on tours, earning himself considerable fees.

In October 1923, only weeks before the murder plan was hatched, Leopold delivered a paper in Boston to the annual meeting of the American Ornithological Union on the Kirtland's Warbler, a rare bird he had sighted.

ing. He had an impaired thyroid and a nervous ailment of blood vessels. Later, he became diabetic.

Intellectually, Nathan Jr made his mark early in life by – reputedly – saying his first words when only four months old.

Glib student

Richard Loeb was born on 11 June 1905 in Chicago, the son of a Roman Catholic mother, Anna, and Jewish father, Albert, who became vice-president of the Sears Roebuck domestic products company. 'Dickie' Loeb was the third of their four sons.

Like Nathan Leopold, Loeb attended the University of Chicago Laboratory School, a preparatory school for bright children, where Loeb showed a quite different type of academic distinction to Leopold. Where Leopold was serious, a genuine scholar, Loeb was brilliant but superficial, finding study an easy matter, and passing examinations glibly and with little depth of thought.

UPI/Bettmann Newsphotos

Richard Loeb (left), dressed as a cowboy and looking like any other young boy. His play, however, was strictly controlled by his governess.

ARRESTED GROWTH

The psychiatrists who examined Loeb in prison after his arrest found that his voice, though mostly 'broken', was still changing and had not fully formed. He did not need to shave every day and suffered from a number of nervous tics indicating a well of bottled-up tension. These included facial tremors and occasional stammering. Another abnormality was that, at 18, he had three baby teeth.

Like Leopold, Richard Loeb had been a physically weak child when very young, but did not suffer any serious ailments. He was never sexually precocious, and appears to have learnt very little about the sexes from either of his parents, who treated their sons indulgently and gently, but in a slightly distant way, lacking intimacy.

Both: New York Daily News

The palatial Chicago mansions of the Loebs, on Hyde Park (above), and the Leopolds, on Greenwood Avenue (right), attested to the great wealth of these two families. The Loeb house was diagonally across the street from the home of the murder victim, Bobby Franks.

Neither boy was an only child, which might have explained some degree of alienation. On the contrary, they came from happy families with normally affectionate children and parents. While Leopold was being questioned day and night for many hours at a stretch, his brother Mike sat outside the interview room, not once contemplating that he abandon 'Babe' at his time of need. Loeb, too, was well supported by his family. His father, who himself had had a very severe upbringing, was, perhaps in response to his own experiences, a tolerant father.

Malevolence

In both cases, the surrendering of parental care to a governess had some malevolent influence upon the children. The governess who had the most important effect on Leopold's development was Mathilda Wantz, or 'Sweetie' as she liked to be called. Her seduction of her young charge introduced him to perverted sexual ideas, possibly bondage and masochism, which directly led to his wishing to repeat the experiences with a master, and to his abject subservience to Loeb.

She gave him abnormal ideas about sex, about stealing and being secretive, and about the concepts of right and wrong.

In Loeb's case, the governess with the most significant influence was a 28 year-old Canadian, a Miss Struthers, who came to look after the young Loeb when he was four years old. Although she never used corporal punishment, she had very definite ideas about discipline and obedience: her practices were so restrictive and demanding that he hardly had pleasures that were not ordained by her, and this led to his indulgence in fantasy and the notion of being powerful enough to escape her domination. He became the 'Superman' of Nathan Leopold's imagination, while Leopold became his adoring slave.

Interviews after his arrest revealed the tactics Loeb developed to cope with the strictness of his governess. 'To get by her, I formed the habit of lying,' he said.

The case showed once and for all that social deprivation was not the only cause of crime. Leopold and Loeb had everything and threw most of it away.

The Perfect Crime

KEY DATES

21 MAY 1924
(all times approximate)

11.00 a.m.	Leopold meets Loeb after classes
11.30 a.m.	Hire of car, and purchase of acid and rope
2.30 p.m.	Leopold and Loeb drive to Harvard School
2.45 p.m.	Pair drive around Kenwood district
5.30 p.m.	Return to Harvard School, Bobby Franks lured into car
5.31 p.m.	Murder of Bobby Franks
8.00 p.m.	Body of Bobby Franks left in culvert by Wolf Lake
10.30 p.m.	Leopold and Loeb play cards

Investigators listened with disbelief as two teenagers from a wealthy district coldly explained how they had killed for thrills to show their superiority over the common mass of people.

It had been in November 1923 that Richard Loeb had first begun to plan the perfect crime. He decided this was possible if prepared by a brain superior to those charged with investigating it. Loeb decided he needed an accomplice.

Nathan Leopold fitted the bill admirably. His study of the 19th century German philosopher, Friedrich Nietzsche, had left him enthralled by the notion of the 'superman' whose actions were outside ordinary considerations of morality and who had his own private code of right and wrong. Loeb himself was obsessed by detective fiction.

Loeb said in his confession that 'the plan was broached by Nathan Leopold, who suggested it as a means of having a great deal of excitement, together with getting quite a sum of money.' Both young men tried to place the greater responsibility on the other. Loeb, however, was the enthusiast about crime.

Leopold had been close to being in love with Loeb, whom he found irresistibly charming, a mixture of sharp mind, easy company and startling

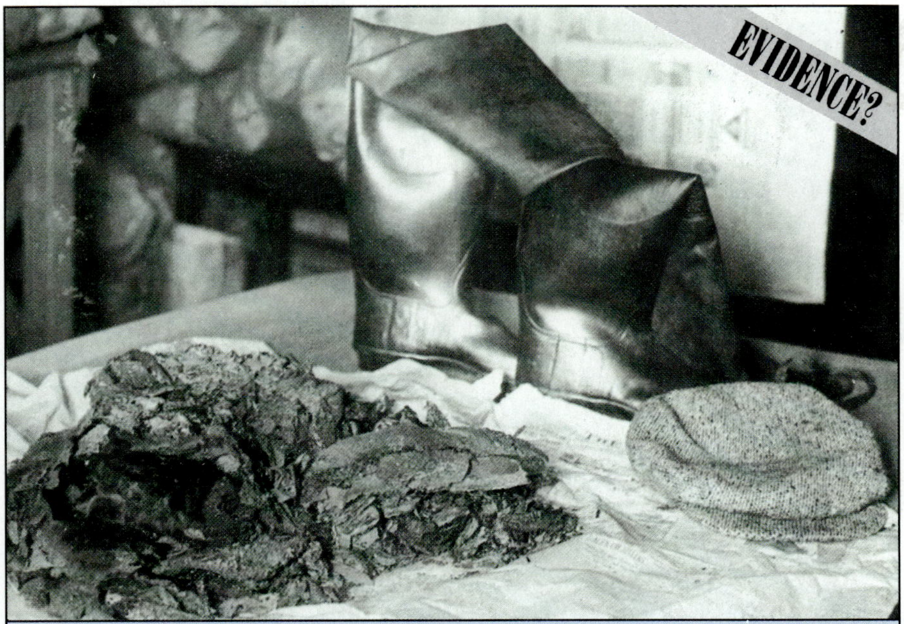

GIVEAWAY CLUES

The 'perfect crime' turned out to be the work of children. Leopold and Loeb left clues at almost every stage of their crime. Shop staff clearly recalled the young men who had purchased the chisel, the rope, the hydrochloric acid and the writing paper used for the ransom letter to Mr Franks. A rail employee identified Loeb as the person who bought a ticket for the Michigan train. One of the victim's stockings was found near the culvert at Wolf Lake. The note was found in the train and the broken parts of the Underwood typewriter were found in Jackson Park Lagoon, where Leopold and Loeb had thrown them on the day after killing Bobby Franks.

Bobby Franks' charred and blood-soaked coat (above) was discovered by Lake Michigan where it had been dumped, and later used as evidence at the trial. Also found were Leopold's boots and cap (above), which he had been wearing during the murder and disposal of the body.

Left: UPI/Bettmann Newsphotos; right: AP/Wide World

AP/Wide World

Fearful that all the power of the family millions would be unleashed in the defence of the accused, State's Attorney Crowe had both Leopold and Loeb pose in the murder car (above left), to rally public opinion against them. Feelings ran high in Kenwood when the coffin containing the body of Bobby Franks (left), surrounded by a massive tribute of flowers, was laid to rest.

conversation. To Leopold, Loeb also possessed loyalty and beauty. He was captivated and would do anything for the younger man who played on Leopold's adoration and allowed him sexual pleasure in return for Leopold's complicity in planning the perfect crime.

Leopold told State's Attorney Crowe about the 'problems' of finding someone to kill. 'This was left undecided to the day,' he said. 'We decided to pick the most likely-looking subject that came our way.'

Crowe was chilled by how unfeeling Leopold sounded. This statement was also one of the first indications that Leopold and Loeb had murdered for the sake of committing murder. They appeared to have borne Bobby Franks neither malice nor sympathy. Leopold and Loeb revealed how they had spent weeks discussing what qualifications the victim's family should have.

IN CONTEXT

TOUGH PROSECUTOR

The man who destroyed the flimsy alibis of Leopold and Loeb was a combative lawyer-politician named Robert E. Crowe, the State's Attorney for Cook County, where the murder was committed. A 45 year-old with Irish roots, a jutting jaw and the nickname of 'Fighting Bob', Crowe was a seasoned campaigner who recognized the depth of public outrage over the killing of Bobby Franks.

Crowe was born in Peoria, Illinois, in 1879 and graduated from Yale Law School in 1901. A member of the Republican Party, he was elected successively as an Assistant State's Attorney and a Chief Justice. An ardent supporter of capital punishment, Crowe ran for office as State's Attorney in 1920 with the slogan, 'To make life, children and property safe in Cook County, vote for Judge Robert E. Crowe.' He mounted a campaign for reelection in the autumn of 1924.

The father had to be wealthy enough to pay a ransom, and the victim had to know and trust Leopold or Loeb, otherwise he could not be lured into their car.

'When was the plan finally effected whereby you considered the Franks boy?' Crowe asked.

'When we saw him – by pure accident,' Leopold replied.

The two rich boys had even considered kidnapping one of their own fathers, but finally decided that, after preparing the ground, they would drive to Harvard School on a given date and select a boy at the last moment.

New identities

In the months before the killing, they opened separate bank accounts under assumed names, and Leopold established a credit line under a false name with a car-hire firm. The pair registered in hotels, using their assumed names to create an identity and history for the characters they were pretending to be.

The two boys agreed on a plan to kill by strangulation so that responsibility for the murder would be shared equally. They agreed on the culvert near Wolf Lake as a hiding place, little suspecting that the body would be discovered before there was time to secure a ransom payment.

The victim's father was to be summoned by telephone to the drugstore on 63rd Street, where he would receive a further message by telephone, instructing him to board a train and look for a piece of paper in the rack of a specified carriage. This slip of paper would tell the father to throw the cigar-box containing the ransom of $10,000 from the moving train at a precise location. There, Leopold or Loeb would retrieve it.

On an Indiana roadside, while police wait and watch, Loeb (centre) searches for the belt of his victim. This was the only item the boys made no attempt to hide.

Crowe, with his long experience, listened to what Leopold and Loeb had considered to be a plan for the perfect crime, but did not comment. His questions explored the randomness of the plan, down to the letter to the victim's father, typed by Leopold the day before the murder, when the victim's identity was still undecided.

'The address you placed on later?' Crowe asked.

'Yes,' Leopold replied. 'It was not addressed inside. It was just "Dear Sir".'

Final details

On the following day, Wednesday, 21 May, Leopold attended a university class in the morning. At 11 a.m. he and Loeb drove downtown to the car-hire firm where Leopold was registered. They selected a dark blue saloon car and drove back to the South Side, where they stopped to buy a quick lunch and to purchase some hydrochloric acid and a length of rope, in case it was needed. In their confessions, Leopold said Loeb had wrapped tape around the blade of a chisel they were carrying. Loeb said

Above & right: Hulton Deutsch Collection

A detective points to stains on floorboards taken from the car hired by Leopold and Loeb, who had lied to police in an attempt to conceal their use of the car at the time of the murder.

Leopold had done it.

At 2.30 p.m. they drove close to Harvard School and parked on Ingleside Avenue. Loeb mooched around, chatting to some associates near the school playground. Leopold got out of the car and whistled for him to return, muttering something about 'possible prospects' nearby.

The two scouted around in the car and on foot for over two hours. At 5 p.m., slightly disconsolate, they drove down Greenwood Avenue, past the Leopold mansion, then turned right back on to Ellis Avenue. 'We caught a glimpse of Robert Franks coming south,' Loeb told the investigators.

> **I teach you the superman. Man is something to be surpassed**
> FRIEDRICH NIETZSCHE

The dark blue car pulled up on Ellis Avenue soon after Bobby Franks had crossed East 49th Street. The boy was enticed into the car to look at a tennis racket. Leopold and Loeb differed in their accounts of what happened next. Leopold said that, while he was driving, Loeb hit Bobby Franks with a chisel, and placed a handkerchief over his mouth. 'Apparently the boy died instantly,' Leopold said, without a trace of feeling.

Loeb claimed he was the driver. 'Leopold grabbed his mouth and hit him over the head with the chisel,' Loeb said. 'He then took one of the gags and gagged him.'

Dead passenger

The body of Bobby Franks was left on the floor of the car as Leopold and Loeb drove east to Jackson Park, then steered on to US Highway 12 along the edge of Lake Michigan. In open country, they halted, checked to see no cars were approaching, and took off most of the dead boy's clothes. These were left in the car but, for no apparent reason, the belt was thrown into the road.

They then drove around, with the child's body still in the car. At the town of Hammond, Indiana, Loeb waited in the car while Leopold went to buy hot dogs and root beer.

After dark, they drove to Wolf Park and removed the rest of Bobby Franks' clothes. 'To render identification more difficult, we poured hydrochloric acid over the face and body,' Leopold said. The body was left inside a culvert.

Burnt evidence

Leopold and Loeb left some of the boy's clothes in the swamp, washed themselves and bundled up the rest of the clothes. 'Apparently at this point the glasses fell from my jacket,' Leopold said.

On East 47th Street, Leopold made the 'Johnson' telephone call that informed Mrs Franks that her son had been kidnapped. Leopold also telephoned his father to say he would be late home. The ransom letter was posted. At Loeb's house, they burnt the rest of Bobby Franks' clothes, and tried to clean up the floor of the hire car. At 10.30 p.m. they went to Leopold's house and played cards.

BACKGROUND

TWO ACCUSERS

Once their guilt was unmasked, any loyalty between Leopold and Loeb was shattered and their pact to share responsibility for the killing was in tatters. After Loeb's confession was read to him, Leopold said in his former friend's presence, 'I was driving, not Mr Loeb, and Mr Loeb was in the back seat. It was Mr Loeb who struck him with the chisel, not I . . . it was his plan and it was he who did the act.'

Loeb, listening to this, vehemently returned the accusation. State's Attorney Crowe asked who wielded the chisel. 'He did,' Loeb said, pointing, 'Nathan Leopold Jr.' Loeb went on to say that Leopold was sitting in the front seat, then corrected himself, saying, 'I am getting excited.' Loeb said the plan to use ether against 'this Franks boy' was formed by Leopold, the scientist.

Facing Leopold, Loeb said, 'I thought that you at least, if the worst comes to the worst, would admit what you had done.'

Leopold replied, 'Those are all absurd, dirty lies.'

IN FOCUS

TRAIL OF CLUES

The killers took their victim in broad daylight. Leaving a long trail of clues, the boys drove a reckless course through city and countryside. Their 'perfect crime' had fast become a mad bungle.

UPI/Bettmann Newsphotos. Above: Chris Lyon

Prosecuting Attorney Robert Crowe (far left) and investigators into the case examine the stolen Underwood typewriter used to write the ransom note. After the murder, Leopold and Loeb had thrown the incriminating machine into Jackson Park Lagoon (right). Loeb (inset right, circled) helps detectives by pinpointing where it was thrown in. Using a magnetic device, divers located it on the bed of the lagoon. The typewriter was a key piece of evidence. Its make, which was clearly visible, was an important factor in its identification.

Hulton-Deutsch Collection. Inset: UPI/Bettmann Newsphotos

THREE

THE TRAIL

A City Seeks Revenge

An outraged community called for Leopold and Loeb to pay the ultimate penalty for their senseless crime. In desperation, their families hired the one lawyer who might win them a measure of pity.

The trial of Nathan Leopold and Richard Loeb on charges of murder and kidnapping opened at Cook County Criminal Court on Monday, 21 July 1924 before Judge John Caverly.

Both charges carried the death penalty. State's Attorney Crowe led the prosecution team and the defence was presented by the celebrated 67 year-old lawyer Clarence Darrow, renowned for his eloquence and opposition to capital punishment.

At 9.30 a.m. the shuffling, shabby figure of Darrow entered the tiny, stifling courtroom, packed with journalists. Leopold and Loeb, dressed in dark suits with their hair slickly combed, sat quietly, the focus of everyone's attention. Their faces showed no sign of remorse or fear. Privately, both believed they would be hanged.

Darrow rose and told the judge that he and his assistants did not believe that either Leopold or Loeb were fit to be released. His next words created more of a surprise. 'We believe they should be permanently isolated from society.' He entered a plea of guilty by both defendants on each charge.

Crowe objected. He had separated the indictments so that if he could not secure a death penalty on the murder, he could proceed with a second trial on the capital offence of kidnapping.

Mitigation

Darrow announced that the facts were not in dispute, and that he intended to present evidence about the state of mind of the defendants, in mitigation. This also meant that Leopold and Loeb would not give evidence. If they had spoken of their crimes in public with the same unfeeling coldness of their confessions, the public disgust with them would have increased.

Darrow's tactics were designed to ensure that Judge Caverly – whom he respected – was the only person who would decide whether to sentence Leopold and Loeb to death. He feared that a jury might be prejudiced.

'If there is any contention they are insane,' Crowe said, 'I ask your honour to call a jury.' One of Darrow's co-counsels, Benjamin Bachrach, said the defence was not claiming that Leopold and Loeb were insane, only abnormal. The judge allowed Clarence Darrow's request.

The hearing of evidence began on Wednesday, 23 July and lasted nearly a month. Crowe had decided to present the fullest possible case against Leopold and Loeb, despite the plea of guilty, and called over 80 witnesses. Darrow cross-examined only one of them.

One of Crowe's assistants, Thomas Marshall, told the court that the legal precedents of the state of Illinois

Popperfoto

State's Attorney Robert Crowe (far left) in vengeful mood in court, and the arraignment (left) with Leopold and Loeb listening to Darrow.

UPI/Bettmann Newsphotos

BACKGROUND

CLARENCE DARROW

Darrow was born in 1857 in the small agricultural town of Farmdale, Ohio, the son of a furniture maker and undertaker. He studied law at the University of Michigan. During his career he defended more than 50 persons charged with first degree murder, losing only one to the executioner. The Leopold–Loeb case was the only case in which he put in a plea of guilty.

In the following year, 1925, he took on another famous case, defending John Scopes, a high-school teacher, for violating a Tennessee law which forbade the teaching of evolution in State schools because it contradicted the Bible. In this case, known as the 'Monkey Trial' for its examination of the theory that human beings evolved from apes, he had a celebrated encounter with prosecutor William Jennings Bryan, which inspired Stanley Kramer's film *Inherit The Wind.*

In one of his last cases, Darrow's clients were convicted of manslaughter, not murder, and had their prison sentences set at one hour. This was the result of what was called Darrow's 'magnificent compassion'. The defendants were a black family who had resisted eviction from their house in a white neighbourhood by a mob of white residents.

Darrow was known for his free-thinking, liberal views, his siding with the underprivileged and his espousal of scientific rather than religious views.

Darrow died in 1938 at the age of 80. His ashes were sprinkled over Jackson Park Lagoon, where Leopold and Loeb had discarded their typewriter.

KEY DATES

JULY-AUG 24

21.7.24	Trial of Leopold and Loeb for kidnapping and murder starts in Chicago
21.7.24	Defendants plead guilty
23.7.24	Start of prosecution evidence
30.7.24	Clarence Darrow opens case for mitigation
12.8.24	Final defence witness gives evidence
19.8.24	End of prosecution rebuttal evidence. Start of final speeches

allowed minors – which technically Leopold and Loeb were – to be executed. If they were not, Marshall said, no jury could be expected to impose the death sentence in any future case. Darrow treated this comment with scorn.

'If I could ever bring my mind to ask for the death penalty,' Darrow said in his opening speech on Wednesday, 30 July, 'I would do it not boastfully or exultantly or in anger or in hate, but I would do it with the deepest regret that it must be done.'

His next passage developed a central theme of his defence – that the

> **There is not a single act in this case that is not the act of a diseased mind, not one**
> CLARENCE DARROW

fate of two teenagers should not be influenced by the public clamour for revenge. 'I have never seen a more deliberate effort to turn the human beings of a community into ravening wolves and take advantage of everything that was offered to create an unreasoned hatred against these two boys,' Darrow said.

The effect of this speech, delivered slowly, in a low, tremulous voice, was to make the prosecuting counsel appear too eager and vindictive, leaving Darrow to bear the burden of dignity, humanity and deep thought which the case merited.

Background stories

Three of the most eminent psychiatrists in the US gave evidence for the defence. They were Dr William White, President of the American Psychiatric Association and the superintendent of a state-run mental institution in Washington DC, Dr Bernard Glueck, a specialist in criminal psychology based at Sing Sing Prison in New York State, and Dr William Healy, an expert in juvenile delinquency.

White, Glueck and Healy had studied the two defendants' history, character and physical condition, and their testimony showed that, at the very least, an intellectual attachment existed between Leopold and Loeb that was intense and dangerous.

The court heard how Loeb had been brought up by a rigid, authoritarian governess from the age of 11, a woman who managed his life, decided who his friends should be, and how he should spend his leisure hours. Loeb had escaped from her influence by reading crime stories and mixing with older boys.

Loeb was subject to frequent fainting fits, sometimes as many as six in a day, during which he would become

Hulton Deutsch Collection

Lorraine Nathan (above), a former girlfriend of Loeb. Although very backward emotionally as a child, Loeb had sexual relations with women in his teens.

IN CONTEXT

SAID IN SECRET

It was rumoured that evidence as to the defendants' sexual habits and experience had been heard in camera or in chambers, away from the court. This is untrue. In American courts, when such evidence had to be given in detail, with accounts of sexual adventures and of masturbation, counsel for both prosecution and defence moved up to the witness box and listened while the evidence was given in so low a voice that only they and the judge could hear it. This is known in American legal jargon as 'whispered testimony'. The transcripts of such evidence are freely available after the trial.

New York Daily News

Leopold and Loeb were ideal study material for the relatively new science of Freudian psychiatry. 'Alienist' Dr William Healy (left) was called by Darrow for the defence.

rigid and froth at the mouth. He had contemplated suicide. He had become deceitful and unscrupulous, and eventually decided to assert his individuality by committing the perfect crime. This crime had been first a fantasy, then a fixation. The idea had been so removed from normal moral considerations that Loeb had even given thought to killing his younger brother or his father.

Emotional cripple

Loeb's schoolfriends had reported that he was always ready to laugh at other's misfortunes. Darrow depicted him as an emotional cripple stuck at the pre-pubescent stage of fantasy.

Nathan Leopold's story, as it unfolded in court, revealed that he too had been brought up with nurses and governesses. His father unwittingly instilled in the boy the notion that wealth implied superiority. At 14, Leopold had been seduced by a nurse into unusual sexual practices. At the same age, he displayed an excessive intellectual ability.

Leopold had declared himself an atheist in his teens, adopting the philosophy of Nietzsche completely and stating that he was not subject to the ethics required of ordinary people. The doctors also disclosed that Leopold, who had large, protruding eyes, felt ugly and fantasized about being the slave of a superman to whom he would submit in total obedience. Leopold was 15 when he met the handsome Loeb.

Psychiatrists called by the prosecution were examined harshly by Darrow. One had based his evidence solely on his observations of the two defendants in court. Others admitted they had spent only brief periods examining Leopold and Loeb in private. Darrow reserved most of his scorn for one psychiatrist who earned his living giving evidence, and took the witness stand to describe Leopold and Loeb as entirely sane.

These victories, however, were only minor ones for the defence. When the last rebuttal witness for the prosecution left the stand on the afternoon of Tuesday, 19 August, the disgust and abhorrence towards Leopold and Loeb had still to be overcome. They had not pleaded insanity. All would depend on an appeal for mercy to the judge.

Assistant counsels on both sides made their final speeches. The details of Bobby Franks' murder left many in court in tears. Everything depended on the contest of oratory between the two leading counsels, Robert Crowe and Clarence Darrow.

New York Daily News

Flanked by guards, Leopold and Loeb (right) sit quietly in the courtroom where their fate – life or death – would be duly decided.

TALKING POINT

LEGEND OF THE SUPERMAN

A 19th century German philosopher imagined a 'Superman' who had the courage of mind to decide his own actions and fate. Two disturbed students thought they were supermen.

Nathan Leopold's friend, Arnold Maremont, a fellow law student at the University of Chicago, testified in court that he and Leopold often debated philosophy, particularly the ideas of the German thinker Friedrich Nietzsche, who died insane in 1900. Nietzsche is best known for his doctrine of the Superman (*Übermensch* – literally 'Overman'), expounded in *Thus Spoke Zarathustra.*

There is little doubt that this idea influenced Leopold in his decision to help Richard Loeb commit murder. Loeb himself was not an intellectual – his favourite reading was detective fiction – but he stood in awe of Leopold's intellect.

There are some curious similarities between Nietzsche and Nathan Leopold. Both were small, slightly-built, short-sighted, shy and brilliant. Leopold studied 15 languages and spoke five of them fluently. He was the

Leopold's sense of intellectual superiority was further fuelled by the ideas of Nietzsche (above), who wrote: 'To be obsessed by moral consideration presupposes a very low grade of intellect. We should substitute for morality the will to our own end.'

UPI/Bettmann Newsphotos

youngest-ever graduate of the University of Chicago. Nietzsche was a student of philology – the science of languages – and became a professor at the incredibly early age of 24.

Eleven years later, he resigned because of ill health, and spent the rest of his life living in furnished rooms, suffering from eye problems and appalling headaches.

'Great health'

Yet despite this, Nietzsche was an optimist by nature, and once declared that the central ideal of his philosophy could be summarized in two words: great health.

Much of his work was a savage attack on Christian morality. Nietzsche believed Christianity to be a religion of the weak, an attempt to justify feebleness and sickness. He admired strength and ruthlessness. One of his heroes was Cesare Borgia, a cunning politician and soldier who used treachery and murder when it suited his purposes.

Nietzsche talked of going 'beyond good and evil', rising above the 'slave morality' of the masses to the 'master morality' of the few. This summary, however, does little justice to his vision. He was one of the great thinkers of the 19th century.

Just for kicks

Richard Loeb was oddly like Cesare Borgia. A born delinquent, he took up crime at the age of nine, stealing money from the boy next door – not because he needed it but for the 'kick' he got out of having got away with it. He became a shoplifter, knowing that if he was caught, his wealthy father could buy him out of trouble. Like Cesare Borgia, Loeb was handsome, gifted and charming, but not particularly intelligent. He seems to have been one of those odd people who are born with a criminal streak.

Nathan Leopold told Arnold Maremont that he thought Loeb was the incarnation of the Nietzschean superman. 'I tried to tell him that he didn't know what he was talking about,' Maremont said, 'that Loeb was glib, superficial, and lied to impress others. Leopold kept insisting I didn't understand Loeb.'

It is easy to see why the shy, introverted Leopold came to regard Loeb as Nietzsche regarded Cesare Borgia. He was sexually infatuated with Loeb but, even without such feelings, he would still have held Loeb in awe. For Loeb was as natural as an animal or a tree. He was completely lacking in something that Leopold had far too much of – self-consciousness.

Leopold wrote later, 'He was at home with everybody. College presidents or hobos, it was all the same to Dick. He fitted in with everybody, became instantly a charter member of any group.'

In short, Dick was the archetypal 'insider', and

Loeb's lack of honesty and sense of obligation to others and Leopold's Nietzsche-inspired views on common morality proved to be a deadly combination.

Nathan was the archetypal 'outsider'.

Yet it was not wholly a case of Loeb leading Leopold astray. Leopold provided the vital element of intellectual justification for crime, the gospel of 'St Nietzsche'. Leopold and Loeb were influenced by Nietzsche just as surely as Ian Brady, the Moors murderer, was influenced by the Marquis de Sade, or as the American sex killer Ted Bundy was influenced by hard-core pornography.

The anti-pornography campaigner Mary Whitehouse and her supporters regard it as sensible and logical to ban obscene literature and the works of de Sade. Many decent, sensible people agree with her. The question remains whether society would then go on to ban Nietzsche, with his baleful influence on Nathan Leopold.

Hulton-Deutsch Collection

ROLE MODEL

One of history's most notorious evil geniuses, Italian statesman Cesare Borgia (above), was Loeb's hero. Borgia had much in common with Nietzsche's Superman.

In his final speech, Darrow drew attention to this connection, quoting a university professor on Nietzsche: 'Although no perfect Superman has yet appeared in history, Nietzsche's types are to be found in the world's great figures – Alexander, Napoleon – in the wicked heroes such as the Borgias . . . These are the gods of Nietzsche's idolatry.'

AP/Wide World

FOUR

THE PLEA

Last Plea For Mercy

Clarence Darrow reached the peak of his career in a speech of simple, homespun eloquence. He pleaded for mercy for mercy's sake. He pleaded for every quality which Leopold and Loeb had denied their victim.

KEY DATES

AUGUST 1924

22.8.24	Darrow begins final appeal for mercy, claiming there is mob fury against accused
25.8.24	Darrow argues that Leopold and Loeb are mentally diseased
26.8.24	Darrow ends appeal after more than 11 hours

The atmosphere in the packed sixth-floor courtroom was electric when, shortly after 2 p.m. on Friday, 22 August, Clarence Darrow rose to make his final appeal for mercy.

A huge crowd had pressed against the doors of the courtroom to gain entrance for Darrow's speech. Some women fainted in the crush. People forced their way in and several were trampled in the chaos. Bailiffs and sheriffs finally sealed the doors and Darrow, wearing a crumpled suit with a waistcoat and white tie, rose wearily to his feet.

His speech was to last over 11 hours. So dramatic was its delivery, so intense its feeling, that it seemed Darrow was summing up his life's work, pleading not only for Leopold and Loeb but all suffering humanity.

'When the public is interested and demands a punishment, it thinks of only one punishment, and that is death,' Darrow said. 'When the public

UPI/Bettmann Newsphotos

Defence lawyer Clarence Darrow (right), and (above) addressing Judge Caverly during his inspired appeal for mercy.

speaks as one man it thinks only of killing . . . I have seen a court urged almost to the point of threats to hang two boys, in the face of science, in the face of experience, and all the better and more humane thought of the age.'

Darrow paced up and down the small area between counsels' tables and the judge's desk, a thumb in his waistcoat pocket. He dealt with the widespread belief that the Leopold and Loeb families would use their immense wealth to save their sons from the harshest penalty.

No money motive

'We announced to the public that no excessive use of money would be made in this case,' Darrow said. 'We have faithfully kept that promise . . . If we fail in this defence, it will not be for lack of money. It will be on account of money.' Darrow then cleverly used this theme to attack the prosecution's claim that greed for money drove Leopold and Loeb to almost unique cruelty.

'I have never yet tried a case where the State's Attorney did not say it was the most cold-blooded, inexcusable, premeditated case that ever occurred,' Darrow commented. 'They say this was a cruel murder, the worst that ever happened. Poor little Bobby Franks suffered very little. There is no excuse for his killing. If to hang these two boys would bring him back to life, I would say let them go, and I believe their parents would say so too.'

Darrow scorned the notion that Bobby Franks died for a ransom. 'These two boys, neither one of whom needed a cent, scions of wealthy people, killed this little, inoffensive boy to get $10,000? It was not money. It was the senseless act of immature and diseased children.'

The court was quite still as Darrow shuffled to and fro. Judge Caverly was leaning forward, his chin resting on a hand, listening rapt as Darrow tried to portray the car journey during which Bobby Franks was kidnapped and killed as so bereft of sense as to be the work of diseased minds. 'The slightest accident, the slightest misfortune, a bit of curiosity, an arrest for speeding,

BACKGROUND

FEES FIXED

State's Attorney, Robert Crowe, said in court, 'The fathers of these boys have an estimated combined fortune of $15 million and we suppose it will be these millions against the death penalty.' Darrow's friends and foes alike suspected he had been enticed by the prospect of an enormous fee. In fact, he asked the Chicago Bar Association to arbitrate and propose a suitable fee, and agreed to be bound by their decision. The famous psychiatrists who testified for the defence similarly were paid a daily rate like any other witness. Darrow's final net personal earnings from the four-month trial were $30,000. Nobody doubted that he would have offered the same spirited defence had his clients been poor and friendless.

They say we come here with a preposterous plea for mercy. When did any plea for mercy become preposterous in any Tribunal in all the universe?

CLARENCE DARROW

AP/Wide World

UPI/Bettmann Newsphotos

Leopold and Loeb (above) in flippant mood. Their tendency to burst into laughter during proceedings was a callous reaction in the circumstances. The only time they appeared moved was at the mention of the shame they had brought on their families, who stuck by them throughout. Mrs Loeb and son Alan (right) leave the County Jail after visiting Richard.

anything, would bring destruction,' he said. Lifting his arms in despair, he added, 'For what? For nothing.'

Throughout his long speech, Darrow constantly referred to Leopold and Loeb, who were both 19 at the time of their trial, as 'boys', or as 'Dickie Loeb' and 'Babe Leopold' to underline that they had not reached an age of judgement or maturity. He spoke of them affectionately in an effort to remove the stigma of monstrosity. Yet occasionally he turned to stare at them with a world-weary gloom.

Despised outcasts

'Why did they kill little Bobby Franks?' Darrow asked after one such interlude. 'Not for money, not for spite, not for hate. They killed him because somewhere in the infinite processes that go to the making up of the boy or the man something slipped, and those unfortunate lads sit here hated, despised outcasts, with the community shouting for their blood.'

Darrow drew upon the expert testimony of the defence psychiatrists, to show that Leopold and Loeb had been driven by some force beyond their control. But, more than that, he asked Judge Caverly to accept that the mere facts of the case were obvious proof that the defendants were mentally disturbed.

'There is not a sane thing in all of this from the beginning to the end,' he insisted. 'There was not a normal act in any of it, from its inception in a diseased brain, until today, when they sit here awaiting their doom . . .

'I am not pleading so much for

these boys as I am for the infinite number of others to follow, those who perhaps cannot be as well defended as these have been, those who may go down in the tempest without aid. It is of them I am thinking and for them I am begging of this court not to turn backward towards the barbarous and cruel past.'

The elderly lawyer, by now tired with his shoulders bent forward, spoke of the English penal system of the 19th century, when nearly 200 crimes carried the death sentence in order to deter crime. 'What happened?' Darrow asked. 'Nothing.'

Forbidden reading

On the second day of his speech, Monday, 25 August, Darrow explored the defendants' backgrounds, and the books which had fascinated them. He spoke of the misfortunes of wealth. Loeb had had a forceful governess who drove him to study, allowing him little healthy leisure time. The law of Illinois forbade minors to read stories of crime, Darrow said, for fear that their minds could be corrupted. Yet Loeb had never stopped reading crime stories and novels, day after day, week in, week out.

UPI/Bettmann Newsphotos

The enormity of the crime and its consequences can clearly be seen in the faces of Nathan Leopold Sr (left), and of Loeb's uncle, Jacob (right).

Darrow then turned to Leopold's fixation with the 'Superman' imagined by the German philosopher Nietzsche. Although both defendants were academically brilliant, Leopold had forced himself on the public imagination as the more serious, less jaunty than Loeb, and more sinister.

'Your honour, I have read almost everything that Nietzsche ever wrote,' Darrow said. 'He was a man of wonderful intellect, the most original philosopher of the last century . . . Nathan Leopold is not the only boy who has read Nietzsche. He may be the only one who was influenced in the way he was influenced . . .

'Here is a boy at 16 or 17 who is becoming obsessed with these doctrines,' Darrow continued. 'It was not a casual bit of philosophy with him. It was his life. He believed in a Superman. He and Dickie were the Supermen . . . Here is a boy who by day and by night, in season and out, was talking of the Superman, owing no obligations to anyone.'

Darrow portrayed Leopold and Loeb as only outwardly freer, luckier, more privileged than less wealthy, less clever youths. He argued that they had never fully begun to grow up, to distinguish between fantasy and real life, because ease and achievement had come too easily and because the boys had had the misfortune to meet each other.

'These two boys, neither one of them, could possibly have committed this act, except by coming together,' Darrow said. 'It was the act of their planning, their conniving, their believing in each other, their thinking themselves Supermen. Without this they could not have done it.'

Nietzsche, said Darrow with tremendous effect, had been insane for the last 15 years of his life. 'His very doctrine is a species of insanity . . . Nietzsche is taught in our schools, discussed in our classes. There is no secret about it. Your honour, it is hardly fair to hang a 19 year-old boy for the

BACKGROUND

A LETTER HOME

Neither defendant gave any evidence nor made any statement to the court about their feelings or their crime. However, the first stirrings of remorse in Loeb showed in his thoughts about what he had done to his own family, if not to that of his victim. In a letter to his parents from prison, he had written:

'Dearest Mompsie and Popsie,

This thing is all too terrible. I have thought and thought about it, and even now I do not understand it . . . Of one thing I am certain, tho' – and this is I have no one to blame but myself . . .'

In a telling passage, Loeb added that it was 'providential' that he was caught because 'there is no telling how far I might have gone.' In anticipating the danger of possible future crimes, Loeb overlooked the actual horror of what he had already done to Bobby Franks.

DISEASED MINDS

IN CONTEXT

Although Richard Loeb is generally held to have been – outwardly – the moving force in planning and carrying out the murder, the defence psychiatrists seem to have found Leopold the more complex, and possibly more sinister personality. Dr William Healy testified that, 'This crime is the result of diseased motivation . . . it was possible only because Leopold had these abnormal mental trends with the typical feelings and ideas of a paranoic personality . . . anything he wanted to do was right, even kidnapping and murder. There was no place for sympathy and feeling to play any normal part . . . He is right. The World is wrong.'

Loeb was described in evidence by Dr Bernard Glueck as showing 'an absolute absence of any signs of normal feeling.' Loeb, he said, could orientate himself only intellectually. He could not impart any feelings to his surroundings.

Loeb had, in fact, found the psychiatric examination boring, and had even fallen asleep during some sessions. Leopold, conversely, had revelled in the opportunity for hours of analysis.

philosophy that was taught him at the university . . .'

On the third and final day of his speech, with the judge, lawyers, defendants and spectators still rapt, Darrow returned to the theme of mercy for the young, and what he saw as the myth that capital punishment deters potential murderers.

'Perhaps all crimes do not have the same cause, but they all have some cause,' he told the court. 'And people today are seeking to find out the cause. Scientists are studying it. Criminologists are investigating it, but we lawyers go on and on and on, punishing and hanging and thinking that by general terror we can stamp out crime . . .

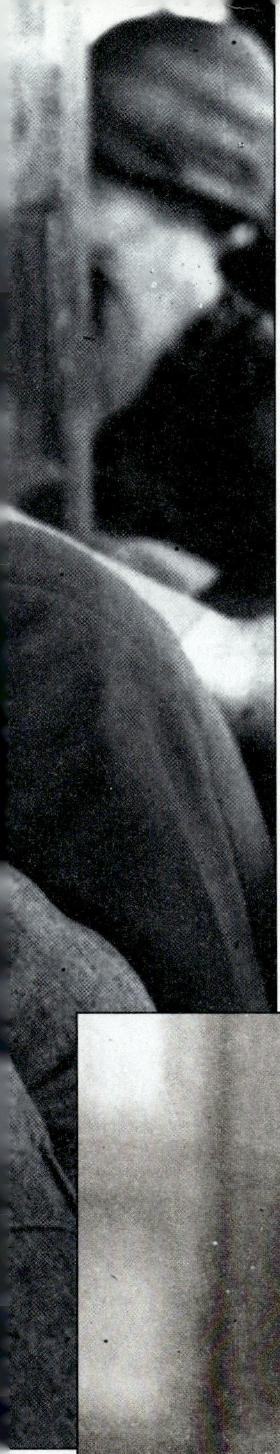

The earnest face of Clarence Darrow (left), in deep conference with his two young clients. Judge John R. Caverly (below) was Chief Justice of the Criminal Court of Cook County, Illinois. Throughout the long trial, he listened to what the attorneys had to say attentively, gravely but impassively, never giving a hint of his true feelings. After the end of this landmark trial, the judge's health was seriously to deteriorate.

'I do not know how much salvage there is in these two boys,' Darrow said sorrowfully. 'I hate to say it in their presence, but what is there to look forward to? I do not know but that your honour would be merciful if you tied a rope around their necks and let them die – merciful to them, but not merciful to civilization and not those who would be left behind.'

> **If the state in which I live is not kinder, more humane, more considerate, more intelligent than the mad act of these two boys, I am sorry that I have lived so long**
>
> CLARENCE DARROW

Leopold and Loeb, sitting a few feet away, had appeared unmoved throughout the trial. The prosecution's portrayal of them as cold-blooded monsters who should hang had not changed their detached, studious expressions. In moments of humour, they had both broken into squeals of high-pitched laughter, but the accounts of Bobby Franks' death elicited no sign of remorse from them. Now, when Darrow spoke of the shame they had brought to their families, Leopold became pale and Loeb began to cry. It seemed that, for the first time, they were confronted with the full shock of destroying their own lives, and causing misery to their families.

Above: UPI/Bettmann Newsphotos; right: AP/Wide World

Plea for mercy

Darrow, close to exhaustion, turned towards Judge Caverly and began his closing speech, in which he acknowledged the powerful tide of public opinion, still calling for full retribution against Leopold and Loeb.

'The easy thing and the popular thing to do is to hang my clients. I know it,' he said. 'Men and women who do not think will applaud. The cruel and the thoughtless will approve. It will be easy today, but in Chicago, and, reaching out over the length and breadth of the land, more and more fathers, the humane, the kind and the hopeful, who are gaining an understanding and asking questions not only about these poor boys but about their own, will join in no acclaim at the death of my clients.

Moved to tears

'I am pleading life, understanding, charity and the infinite mercy that considers all. I am pleading that we overcome cruelty with kindness and hatred with love. I know the future is on my side . . .'

Darrow's voice slowly trailed away into silence. The tired, shambling figure sat down. Two minutes passed without sound in the courtroom. Judge Caverly sat still, weeping.

FATAL PARTNERSHIP

Only by acting in partnership could Leopold and Loeb have committed murder. The chemisty of their two personalities was fatal.

When the Leopold and Loeb case came up for trial in 1924, the Viennese school of psychiatry, pioneered by Sigmund Freud, was relatively new and still excitingly fresh. Nathan Leopold and Richard Loeb, who had apparently killed a young boy known to them both without any reason, without any malice, and without any emotional commitment, were perfect subjects for the Freudians.

Into the mind

No less than 14 'alienists', as psychiatrists were then known, examined the defendants and pored over the interpretation of their dreams and fantasies in an effort to discover the key to how their unconscious minds worked.

They seemed to have murdered intellectually, to prove a point, but the psychiatrists were convinced that the root of their decision to kill must be hidden in childhood sexual imagin-

Topham Picture Source; inset: Hulton-Deutsch Collection

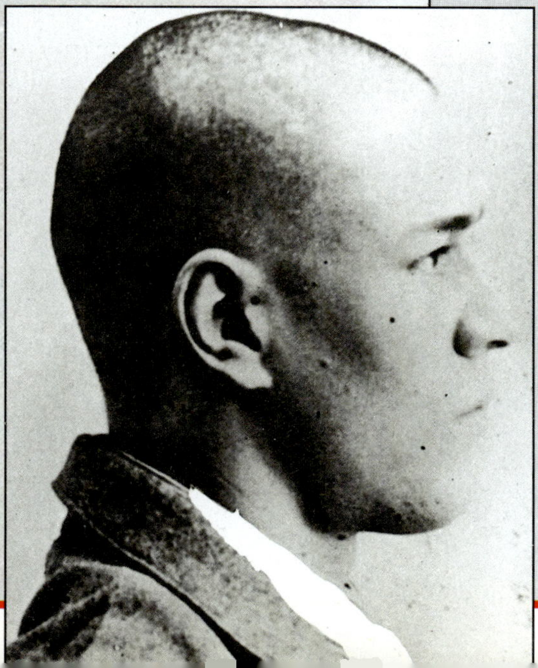

One mad act, the product of an unbalanced mind, turned Richard Loeb from a privileged young man (above left), with a glittering future, into a convicted murderer, Prisoner No. 9305 (inset), doomed to spend the rest of his life behind bars. But 12 years later Loeb too was to be killed.

LOVE AND HATE

Leopold and Loeb each privately considered murdering the other in the final, fevered months before the killing of Bobby Franks. Richard Loeb told two psychiatrists, Dr Karl Bowman and Dr H.S. Hulbert, who examined him in prison before the trial, 'I had always considered him [Leopold] a bad influence upon me,' and admitted planning to kill his friend and make it look like an assault. Loeb said he had abandoned the plan for fear of being an obvious suspect.

Leopold told the same psychiatrists, 'If I could have snapped my fingers and made him pass away in a heart attack, I would have done it.' The intensity of their friendship was so suffocating that each also considered suicide. Loeb shied away from such an act because he felt it was a sign of failure, even when Leopold threatened to kill him for refusing to play a poker game to decide which of them should take his life.

Topham Picture Source; inset: Hulton-Deutsch Collection

The two faces of Leopold (right and inset). He was totally under Loeb's spell and desperately sought his affection and approval.

ings. These imaginings stemmed from their innermost unconscious instincts, which had remained suppressed, and then had risen up to slay Bobby Franks.

They had a difficult task, and it cannot be said they succeeded. Leopold and Loeb baffled psychiatrists of the day and they baffle them still. The most that can be said, though not with certainty, is that Loeb was a schizoid type, afraid of showing emotion lest it be misunderstood or scorned. He was therefore prone to distort and ultimately annihilate the emotional content of his being.

Mixed emotions

In the friendship between the two murderers, it was Leopold who showed genuine emotion, while Loeb was happy to accept his adoration while not necessarily feeling it. It is common also for the schizoid with psychopathic tendencies to be utterly charming and plausible, popular, intelligent, and manipulative, all of which applies to Loeb, who was certainly the initiator of the scheme to commit a perfect crime.

The last significant piece of evidence was that Loeb regretted that he and Leopold were caught, and was sorry for the distress caused to his own family. However he never once showed any remorse for the act of murder itself.

Leopold admitted that he began to feel remorse about ten years afterwards, and that the remorse grew and grew like a cancer within him. He ascribed this to late maturity, and said that at the time of the crime he had been an arrogant young man.

He had been sure of his own superiority, in class, wealth and intelligence, but had longed to be the slave of a greater man. In other words, he was corrupted by praise and his own brilliance, felt apart from the norm, and wanted to belong. Loeb offered him the chance to feel that he was part of a whole, and in gratitude Leopold offered his total obedience.

At their trial, the boys defence could give no evidence of insantiy on a plea of guilty, as the question of insanity had to be decided by a jury, which would only hear a plea of not guilty. The case was heard, therefore, without a jury, and mental disease was allowed to be introduced in mitigation only.

To Live or Die

One judge had the lonely task of balancing justice, law and the protection of a community. Leopold and Loeb sat in jail, day after day, waiting to be told if they were to live or die.

Every newspaper in Chicago printed the whole of Clarence Darrow's speech, as did many throughout the US. Never before had such a tribute been paid to a working advocate. The speech was later published as a pamphlet and became a bestseller. But the trial was not over.

State's Attorney Robert Crowe spoke for two days against Darrow's view of the case, with a maddened fury which no longer quite matched the public mood. He virtually shouted himself hoarse. Leopold and Loeb, he said, were ruthless killers 'as little entitled to sympathy and mercy as a couple of rattlesnakes, flushed with venom, and ready to strike.'

Crowe airily dismissed what he called all the nonsense about fantasies and literature and pacts. The case was simple, he said. Leopold knew something about Loeb and blackmailed him into submission to his sexual desires. They both planned the murder with meticulous thoroughness, over several months, and they both executed it. Neither had shown any remorse. The motive was money – $10,000 to be precise – and to pretend otherwise was idiotic.

Crowe attacked the defendants' wealth, referring to Darrow as a 'million-dollar defence' who had been bought by greed and venality. He also attacked Darrow's personal character. Over and over again he repeated that Darrow was 'an atheist, the same as his clients.' He was 'the exponent of a philosophy as dangerous as Leopold's' and 'a paid advocate whose profession it was to protect murder in Cook County, and concerning whose health thieves inquire before they go out to commit crime.' It was a desperate performance by a man frustrated at winning the case but losing the argument.

Judge Caverly adjourned the trial until September, by which time, he said, he would have reached a decision. To avoid public demonstration or panic, he would bar the court to all but the defendants, their families, their counsel and the press.

> **For the past quarter century remorse has been my constant companion. It is never out of my mind. Sometimes it overwhelms me completely**
>
> NATHAN LEOPOLD in 1957

IN CONTEXT

THE FRONT PAGE

On the day of the sentencing, Chicago newspapers printed two different sets of headlines, one for death, the other for life imprisonment. The latter were on sale within minutes of the sentence being passed. Special editions were published in London 40 minutes later.

An American transcontinental train made a ten-minute stop in a small town in the western state of Montana. When the conductor shouted 'All aboard' the passengers refused to board the train until the sentence came through half an hour later.

The reaction by leading newspapers to the sparing of the defendants' lives varied. But most agreed that Leopold and Loeb should never be released. The mood was expressed by the *Chicago Herald and Examiner*, which commented, 'The public forgets many things, but a murder like this is not one of them, and the public will insist on full atonements.'

Tense wait

On 10 September 1924, upon a trial so much in the public eye, Judge Calverly entered the courtroom at 9.30 a.m. and asked Leopold and Loeb, who sat on either side of a tense Clarence Darrow, if they had anything to say before being sentenced. Loeb shook his head. Leopold quietly said 'No.' The judge announced that it was his duty to explain the reasons for his decision in view of the world-wide

Handcuffed to guards, the two accused (left) are led into the courtroom to hear their sentence, which was to be a mixed victory for State's Attorney Crowe (below, centre).

Both: UPI/Bettmann Newsphotos

KEY DATES

AUG-SEPT 24

25.8.24 State's Attorney Crowe starts two-day speech, demanding death penalty

10.9.24 Judge sentences Leopold and Loeb each to life imprisonment and 99 years for murder and kidnapping

interest in the case. There was no doubt of the defendants' guilt.

The chain of proof would have been overwhelming without the confessions. 'The plea of guilty, therefore, does not make a special case,' Judge Caverly said, rejecting Darrow's first line of argument for mitigation.

> **It is the most terrible criminal offence that has been perpetrated in this generation**
> ROBERT CROWE, State's Attorney

The judge then dealt with the expert medical evidence about the defendants' mental states. The defence had not claimed they were insane, and the judge affirmed that he did not believe that any such case could have been made. Judge Caverly then went on to say that the tests were 'a valuable contribution to criminology' but could have produced similar results in other cases.

The judge acknowledged that Leopold and Loeb were abnormal, commenting, 'Had they been normal they would not have committed the crime.' But he refused to accept Darrow's argument that their abnormality was a mitigating circumstance. He also said the question of ultimate responsibility for human actions was outside the realm of the court, whose task was to apply the law. 'The testimony in this case reveals a crime of singular atrocity,' he continued. 'It is in a sense inexplicable, but it is not thereby rendered less repulsive and inhumane. It was deliberately planned and prepared for during a considerable period of time. It was executed with every feature of callousness and cruelty.'

He made a particular point that there was no evidence the victim had been subject to any sexual molestation, but said that did not make the crime less revolting. 'The court is satisfied that neither in the act itself, nor in its motive or lack of motive, nor in the antecedents of the offenders, can he find any mitigating circumstances,' the judge announced.

Sentenced

The prosecuting counsel looked satisfied. The defendants were correspondingly despondent and Darrow was glum. Caverly read the statutes and listed the punishments laid down.

'It would have been the path of least resistance to impose the extreme penalty of the law,' Judge Caverly said, to murmurs of surprise. 'In choosing imprisonment instead of death, the court is moved chiefly by consideration of the age of the defendants.'

The judge added that his decision not to impose death on 'persons who

IN CONTEXT

LEOPOLD'S CONTEMPT

The final comments made by Nathan Leopold to the press after sentence revealed the depth of his contempt for any group whom he could think of as inferior masses. On 11 September 1924, after one night at the state penitentiary at Joliet, Illinois, the two new prisoners attended a service to mark the national Defence Day. Reporters were present. Later, Leopold commented to the *Chicago Tribune*, 'I suppose this wouldn't be so hard for some dull fellow with not much intelligence, and no imagination, and no real life behind him. That's what makes it hard for Dick and me.' Leopold was still, in his own eyes, Superman.

UPI/Bettmann Newsphotos

After listening to months of evidence and argument, Judge Caverly (left) finally passed sentence. Defendants and defence counsel were surprised but relieved. The prosecution was shocked.

JACQUES MESRINE

Hulton Picture Company

The French dubbed him 'Public Enemy No. 1', but many people secretly admired his daring escapes from prison and cheeky mockery of the police. The legend was hollow. Jacques Mesrine was a vindictive, brutal murderer who felt no remorse for the victims of his private war against civilized society.

ONE

ESCAPE

Strutting Thieves

In the years when France was dismantling its empire, hard, battle-trained adventurers were returning home, embittered by lost territories and with no interest in a routine life. For some, crime with a theatrical flourish was salvation.

On the afternoon of 12 November 1967, a couple walked into the foyer of the Hotel de la Croix Blanche in the French town of Chamonix. The man was tall and powerfully built, with an air of confidence. His female companion was dark-haired with a good-looking, if slightly coarse, appearance.

They took up their reservation for a double room for 10 days and signed the register. The man gave his name as Jean-Jacques Moreau, a 33 year-old company director from Paris. It was an old habit of his not to sign his real name in hotels.

The couple planned to have a simple winter holiday and enjoy a good rest. But, while eating dinner in the hotel two days later, they saw a man at the reception desk who interested them. The guest was an Arab, in western clothes, and looked wealthy.

A waiter explained that the guest was Albert Setruk, who often visited the hotel and was rumoured to carry millions of francs in his briefcase. The couple noticed that while Setruk chatted to the receptionist, the briefcase stood on the floor by his feet. Later, discreet inquiries among the hotel staff revealed that Setruk was Tunisian and frequently visited the town's casino late in the evening.

The Tunisian and his aide, André Flery, went to the casino that very night, returning at about 2 a.m. on the morning of 15 November. The night receptionist was a dark-haired woman whom Setruk did not recognise. She escorted the two men to the lift, explaining to their surprise that their keys were in the doors to their rooms.

As the three emerged from the lift on the first floor, they were confronted by the tall fellow guest. In a moment, a gun was pointing at them. Assisted by the dark-haired girl, the man searched Setruk and Flery, taking their documents and about 7,000 francs. The two men were then pushed downstairs, gagged and bound, and left behind the desk, where they lay beside the trussed-up figure of the more familiar night receptionist.

The thieves cut the hotel telephone wires, loaded their cases into the car, called out a farewell to the three men they had tied up and drove off. Their names were Jacques Mesrine and

Rex Features

I have no remorse at all . . . I feel as if I am robbing an even bigger robber than myself.

JACQUES MESRINE

The younger Mesrine (left) had a look of roguish fun. But his crimes became crueller as his yearning for acclaim, and his fear of capture, grew stronger.

Popperfoto

THE OAS

Many of Mesrine's criminal skills were honed during the early 1960s by the sinister OAS, or *Organisation de l'Armée Secrète.* The OAS was an armed right-wing faction, formed in 1961 to sustain French colonial control over Algeria. At this time many politicians in Paris were calling for a negotiated settlement with the Algerian guerrilla movement, the FLN (above).

The OAS launched a campaign of terror in France and Algeria, using plastic bombs, shootings and extortion to achieve its ends. The OAS could not prevent President de Gaulle, whom it tried to assassinate, from granting Algerian independence in July 1962, but it maintained its worldwide organization.

Mesrine, who had served with distinction in the French army in Algeria, was useful to the OAS as a brazen adventurer when arms had to be smuggled and documents pilfered. He probably first worked undercover for the OAS in 1961 or 1962 and learnt the shooting skills, care in planning and elusiveness that marked his private criminal career.

KEY DATES

MAR 62-DEC 68

3.62	Jailed for first time, after conviction for robbery and firearms offences
7.63	Released from prison on parole
2.12.65	Arrested during theft of political documents in Mallorca and given suspended sentence
15.11.67	Armed robbery at hotel in Chamonix
6.2.68	Leaves for Canada with Jeanne Schneider

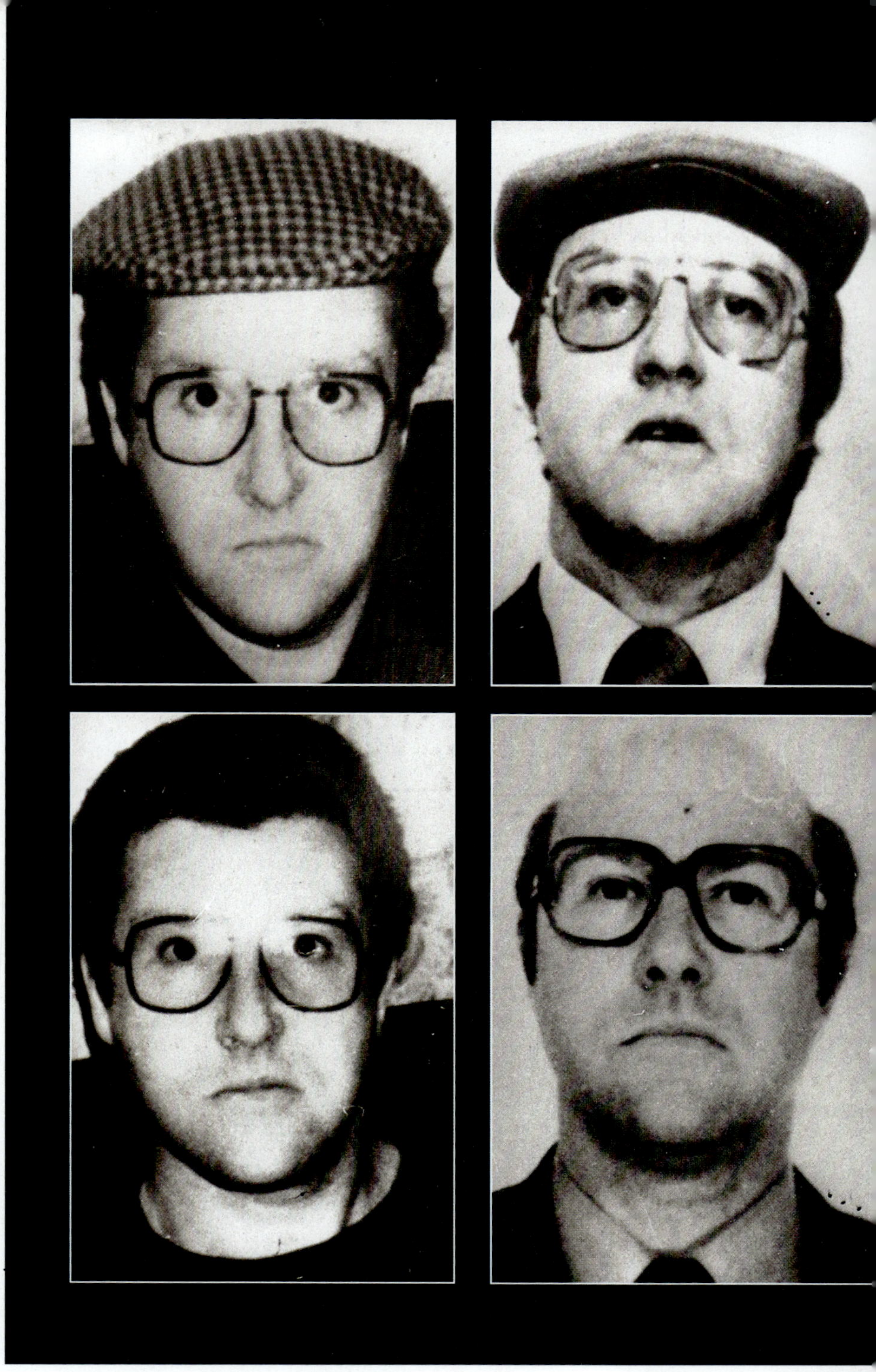

Jeanne Schneider.

Financially, the robbery had not been a great success. Mesrine had found no money inside Setruk's briefcase when he broke into his room. But he was delighted that Schneider seemed to enjoy the sheer thrill of danger. The 29 year-old Mesrine had waited a long time to find a mistress with his own cool.

Showman

Throughout his career, Mesrine had enjoyed brazenly outwitting his opponents. He liked to be conspicuous to the point of flamboyance. In 1960, on his first known robbery, Mesrine had entered a block of flats with a splendid bouquet of flowers. Two years later, he used his father's car to execute a robbery at the home of a wealthy engineer, Robert Grussenbucher, in Normandy. He escaped with jewellery, paintings and cash.

Six weeks later, Mesrine had been arrested while recklessly driving the same car to a different robbery. Police found guns in the car. Mesrine was sentenced to three years' imprisonment. Although released on parole after less than 18 months, it rankled with him that he had not actually escaped from jail.

Now, driving away from Chamonix in the darkness, Mesrine felt that life was doing him justice. He had admired the way Jeanne Schneider had waved the gun in the faces of their victims and laughed when Mesrine had punched Setruk on the chin.

Mesrine and Schneider committed several more thefts over the following weeks. In some, Jeanne dressed as a man. Often, her presence seemed to inspire Mesrine to show off and take unnecessary risks. Their crimes took on a brutal, violent edge and Mesrine developed a habit of lingering too long at the scene of a crime, savouring his triumph.

In one of these, on 8 December 1967, Mesrine, a male accomplice and Jeanne, dressed as a man, bound and gagged a dressmaker named Madame Coudercy, and her daughter and son-in-law, inside her shop in the rue de Seze in Paris. Each of the gang was armed.

Slow torment

Mesrine spent much of the night drinking heavily and recounting his criminal exploits to his terrified victims. He toyed with the dressmaker and her daughter by waving a flick-knife close to their faces. Eventually, the robbers escaped with jewels and valuables worth millions of francs.

Mesrine's taunting violence inside the dressmaker's shop showed a new

IN CONTEXT

THE MISTRESS

Mesrine met his accomplice, Jeanne Schneider, in a nightclub in the Place Blanche, in the Pigalle district of Paris, some time during the late summer or autumn of 1967. She was a prostitute with a criminal record, well known to the 'milieu', the underworld. Mesrine was drawn by her warmth and worldliness, and she by the outrageousness and charm of a villain very different from the more furtive characters with whom she was linked. She initially viewed Mesrine with devoted awe, and became disenchanted only when his later career moved from impudent robberies to callous violence. To Mesrine, Jeanne Schneider was a lover whose attractiveness and daring made her almost the ideal audience for his individual style of crime.

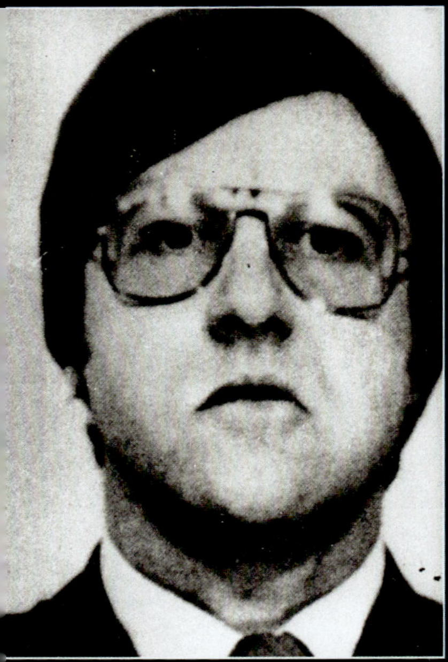

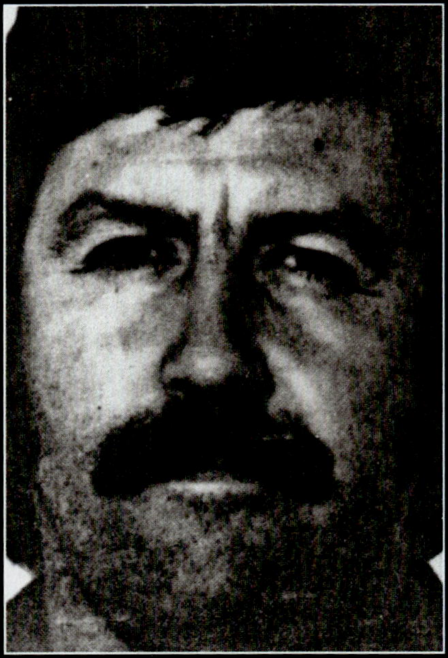

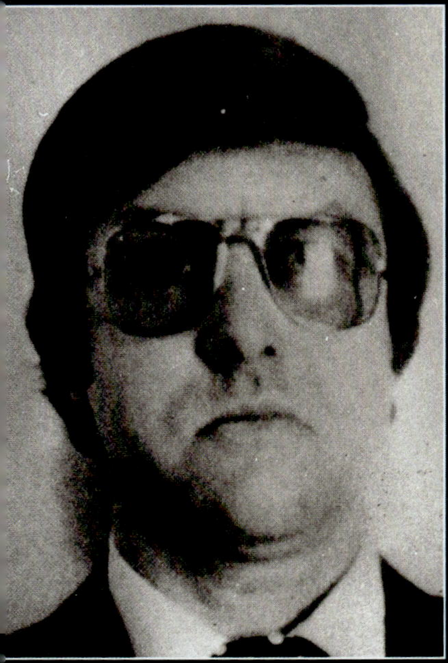

The many faces of Mesrine all seemed to laugh at the camera. Despite his use of glasses, caps and different hairstyles (above), he made little attempt to disguise the shape of his head or brazen expression. All strongly resemble the real man (below). Mesrine much preferred to be recognized as himself.

IN CONTEXT

SECRET PAPERS

One of Mesrine's most freakish adventures ended in his arrest on 2 December 1965 inside the Palma home of the Governor of Mallorca. He told the local officers of the Guardia Civile that he was an ordinary thief hired by an anonymous intermediary to steal certain documents. The Guardia, learning that these papers were top-secret, assumed Mesrine must be a French government agent and sent him to Madrid for questioning by the French ambassador. No one believed Mesrine's insistent and true denials that he was an official French agent and his case was hurried through the courts in order to avoid embarrassment to the French government. Mesrine, who received a suspended six-month prison sentence, is believed to have undertaken the burglary for the OAS.

side to his criminal style, which had previously expressed itself as a combination of bravado and straightforward aggression.

The police in Paris and across France compiled detailed reports of Mesrine's bravado. He soon turned from a man merely under suspicion and wanted for questioning into a fugitive. After brief trips to Spain and Italy, Mesrine and Jeanne Schneider decided to escape from the pressure of a manhunt in their own country. Early in 1968, they caught a flight to Montreal in Canada. It was five years before Mesrine saw France again, and during that time his criminal career grew broader and deeper.

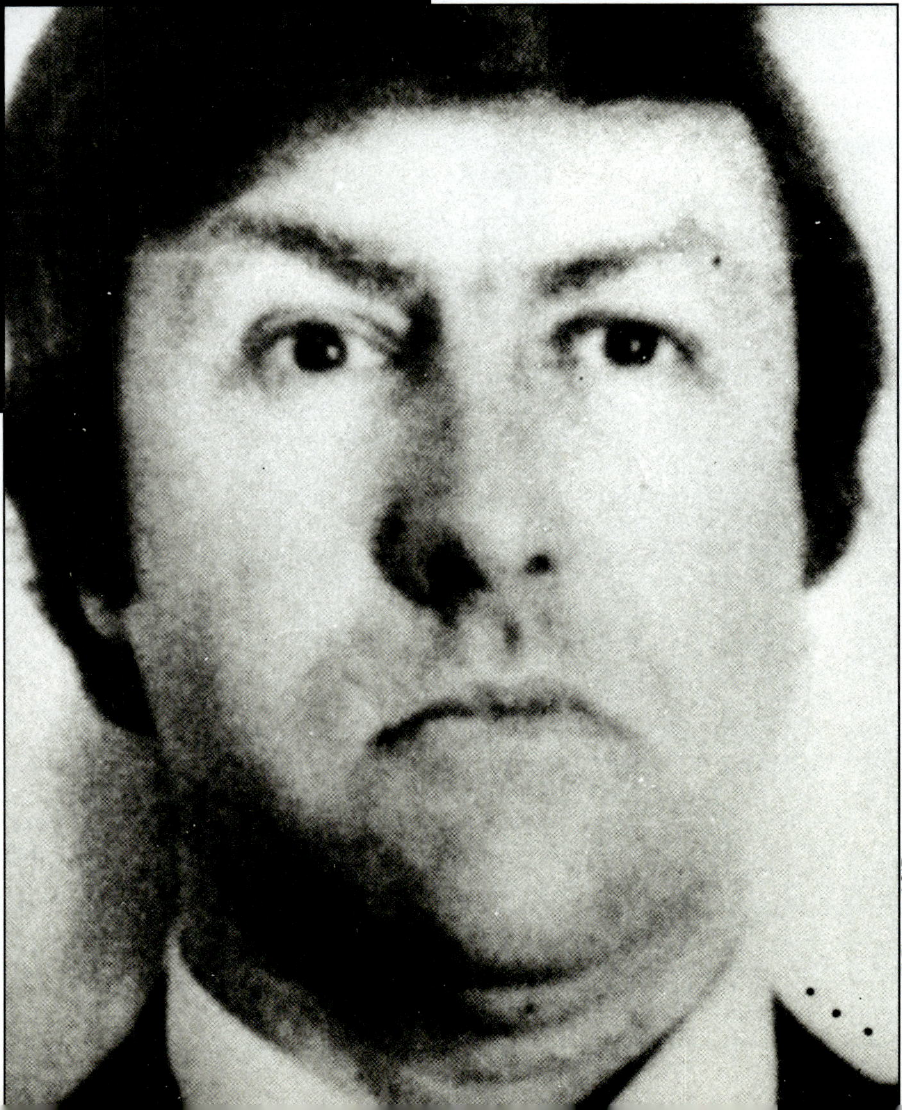

All Pictures AGIP

THE CHILD OF WAR

Mesrine grew up in an occupied country where people argued about the meaning of victory and bravery.

AGIP

Jacques Mesrine was born into a comfortable, middle-class family on 28 December 1936. His father, Pierre, ran his own business designing textiles while his mother, Monique, provided a warm home life for Jacques and his elder sister in their apartment in Clichy, on the northern outskirts of Paris.

In June 1940, at the outset of World War II, Pierre Mesrine entered the French army as Monique and the children joined the throng of refugees fleeing from Paris. They travelled south to Chateau-Merle, a village near Poitiers, where they stayed with relatives. Soon, Paris fell to the German army and Mesrine's father was held in a prison camp.

The boy Mesrine spent three rather solitary years in Chateau-Merle. After some time his mother had returned to occupied Paris to look for work and her son, though liked for his charm, often chose to play or wander by himself rather than join other boys. 'I have a nicer time on my own,' he told a concerned adult.

Inner conflict

The only men in their prime around the village tended to be full-chested German soldiers and the stealthy, conspiratorial members of the French Resistance who crept around the houses at night. These two extremes pre-figured Mesrine's own adult life – the strutting, show-off villain and the shadowy outlaw on the run.

The Mesrine family was reunited after the war in 1945 and settled once again in Paris. After being left much to his own devices in the countryside, the eight-year-old Jacques found the discipline of school life constrictive. But he performed well enough and, at the age of 12, was sent to a boarding school in Juilly, some 50

As a youth, Mesrine (above) grew up in the so-called unoccupied zone of France governed by Marshall Pétain (right).

Popperfoto

kilometres (30 miles) away. Here, tempted by the freedom, he became a troublemaker and in the summer of 1951, he was expelled.

By this time, the family had bought an old farmhouse in Normandy for weekend retreats. Jacques borrowed a rifle from a neighbour and learnt to shoot, though he later declared that he shot mainly at trees or milk bottles. The youth loved animals and spent long, solitary hours studying the wildlife.

Fighting drudgery

These ruminative periods were in direct contrast to his life in the bustling city of Paris where he had signalled a need to be famous without a willingness to work patiently for success.

Reading the warning signs, Pierre Mesrine sent his son to a local school, Lycée Chaptal, but Jacques soon slipped into truancy, leaving his school books with a friendly café owner before going off to a cinema or to meet a girlfriend. When he did attend school, Mesrine often spoiled for a fight, apparently needing to test his strength or his sharp-wittedness in debate rather than to inflict pain.

The inevitable expulsion from Lycée Chaptal was followed by an abortive attempt to complete an electronics course at a technical college.

Menial jobs

Without any qualifications, Mesrine had no choice but to take menial jobs, which he hated. But during this period he met and married a beautiful girl called Lydia from Martinique in the West Indies. She was already pregnant, but Mesrine seemed unconcerned at becoming the father of another man's child. They moved into a tiny flat where Mesrine, already a gourmet, enjoyed having his own kitchen. He also enjoyed the company of Lydia's easy-going family, who did not make demands on him. But he was annoyed that Lydia gave up her university course in chemistry, because he had hoped to depend on her earnings.

Troubles at home

Lydia, in turn, resented Mesrine's growing disinclination to take on a proper job. The rows soon started and, when Lydia's child was born, Mesrine found that he resented having to provide for him. Soon the novelty of the new family started to wear off and Mesrine began to neglect his wife.

It was a relief to the young man, still only 19, when his army call-up papers arrived in the autumn of 1956. Very soon, he volunteered for active service in Algeria, the French colony where the army was fighting to quell a nationalist uprising.

Popperfoto

Mesrine had three children by his second wife – two boys and a girl, Sabrina (above). Although he abandoned his family to pursue a life of crime, Sabrina remained devoted to her father and was devastated when he finally met his death at the hands of a team of police marksmen.

Mesrine's mother, Monique (below), was a hardworking housewife. Her appeals to Mesrine to avoid trouble were ignored.

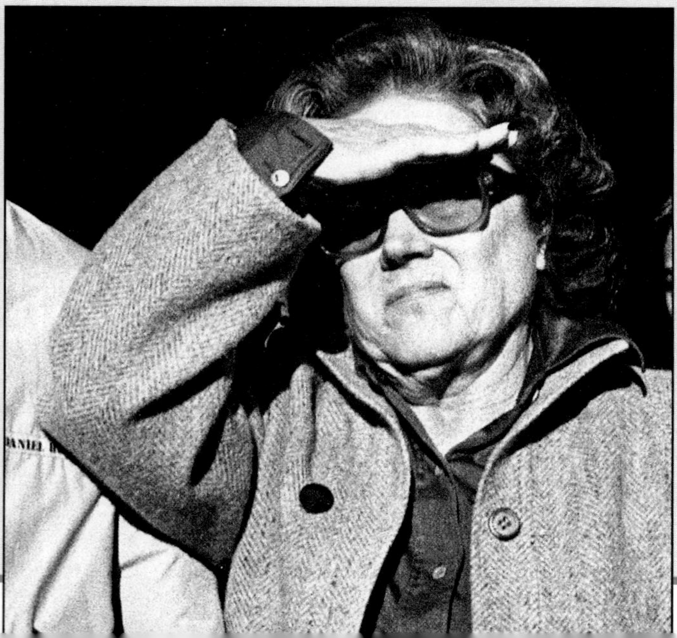

Popperfoto

MARRIAGE

Mesrine's second wife, Soledad, a Spanish girl with raven hair, was as implacably opposed to his life of crime as his first wife, Lydia, had been. The couple met while Mesrine was spending a holiday in the Costa Brava in 1960. A year later, Soledad gave birth to their first child, Sabrina.

Soledad tried everything from quiet patience to outbursts of rage to lead Mesrine away from crime, but to not the slightest avail. The couple were married in the winter of 1961 and Soledad was waiting with Mesrine's parents at the prison gates in Orleans when he was freed from his sentence for robbery in July 1963. A son, Jacques, was born late the next year and a second son followed in the spring of 1966. Although Mesrine doted on the children, particularly his daughter, he could no longer stand Soledad's pleadings. It was only as a criminal that he displayed the attributes of which he was proud. In the summer of 1966, Mesrine left his family without farewells. Soledad eventually returned to Spain and the children were brought up by Mesrine's mother.

TWO

THE MURDERS

Breaking Out

KEY DATES

MAR 69-SEP 72

4.69 Mesrine and Schneider kidnap Georges Deslauriers
30.6.69 Body of Evelyne Le Bouthillier found at motel in Percé
23.7.69 Mesrine and Schneider escape briefly from prison
8.69 Pair jailed for 10 and five years respectively for Deslauriers' kidnapping
1.72 Mesrine and Schneider acquitted of murdering Madame Le Bouthillier
21.8.72 Mesrine escapes from top-security jail
3.9.72 Mercier and Mesrine shoot and kill two forest rangers

Mesrine and his new accomplice made a quiet start to their new life across the Atlantic. Then all restraint went by the board in a crazed spate of sensational crimes that made the Frenchman one of the most vilified crooks in the world.

Mesrine did not immediately resume his criminal activities in Canada. He took a job on a building site and, when this work finished, he found work as a chauffeur. He wanted to study the lie of the land before committing himself to risky ventures.

Mesrine's first crime in the New World owed more to opportunism and revenge than to planning for gain. On 7 March 1969, he and Jeanne had entered the service of Georges Deslauriers, a wealthy but crippled businessman who could walk only with the aid of crutches. Mesrine was to act as chef and chauffeur, while Jeanne was to be the housekeeper. The couple were housed in the lodge on Deslauriers' large, picturesque estate at Saint-Hilaire, on the outskirts of Montreal.

Sacked

There is no proof that Mesrine intended from the outset to rob his employer. However, following a violent quarrel between Jeanne and another of the servants, the French couple were asked to leave. Jacques was filled with resentment as he always was when dismissed or excluded.

The pair returned to Montreal, where Mesrine hatched a plan to kid-

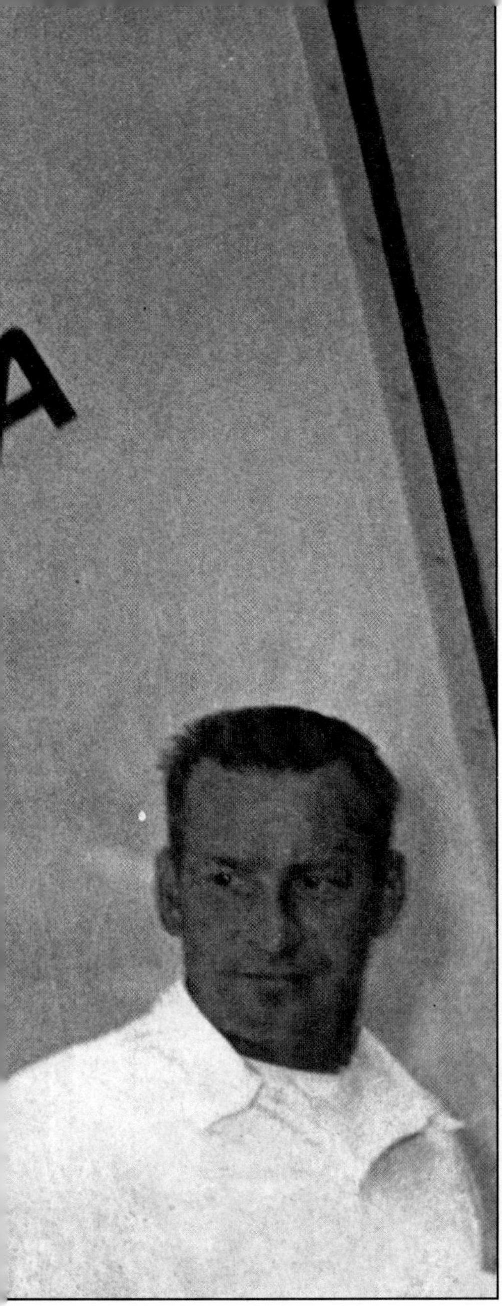

Publication Police Photo

ALLO Police

Mesrine chats amiably to Jeanne Schneider (above) as they arrive in Canada, just weeks before they embark on crimes which send shock waves through the country.

nap Deslauriers and hold him to ransom. For this scheme, he enlisted Michel Dupont, a young Frenchman, and Jeanne drove them to the estate after midnight, an hour when the helpless landowner would be alone.

Deslauriers was bundled into the car and driven away. Mesrine delivered a ransom note to his brother, demanding 200,000 Canadian dollars, but the brother did not appear at the designated venue and the kidnappers, returning to their flat, found that their captive had escaped. The three fled to the port of Percé, some 800 kilometres (500 miles) away. Dupont was arrested when, foolishly, he returned to his home in Montreal.

BACKGROUND

THE KIDNAP

Mesrine's first attempt at kidnapping was a fiasco. His former employer, Georges Deslauriers, a wealthy 69 year-old cripple, was abducted in his bedroom by Mesrine, who held a knife, and Jeanne Schneider, armed with a revolver. He was ordered to write a note to his brother Marcel. This began: 'I will be killed unless I can find 200,000 dollars . . .' On Mesrine's orders, Deslauriers also wrote a note explaining that he had been called away on business. This was pinned to the front door by the kidnappers to deter callers to the house.

Deslauriers was left on his own at Mesrine's flat in Montreal and, in spite of his disability, managed to find his crutches, which had been taken away from him, after crawling through the rooms. He escaped safely. Mesrine had given the elderly gentleman a drugged drink but this had apparently had little effect on him.

During Mesrine's brief stay at the Three Sisters Motel in Percé (above), he charmed the owner, Evelyne Le Bouthillier (right). But when he left she was dead. He was cleared of her murder.

ALLO Police. Above: Publication Police Photo

While in Percé, the kidnappers stayed at the Three Sisters Motel, posing as Belgian tourists and befriending the owner, Madame Evelyne Le Bouthillier. She invited them into her room for drinks. On 29 June 1969, over a week after Dupont's departure, Mesrine and Schneider booked out of the motel and headed towards Quebec province. The next morning, Madame Le Bouthillier was found strangled.

Shortly afterwards, Mesrine and his mistress crossed the US border in a hired car and drove south. On Dupont's information, they were arrested just outside Dallas, Texas, and, on 23 July 1969, flown back to Montreal to face charges for both the Deslauriers kidnapping and the murder of Madame Bouthillier. Mesrine vehemently denied the murder charge, expressing outrage at being accused of killing a helpless woman.

Pending the trial, Mesrine was held in prison back in Percé and may well have decided that the comparative lack of security there presented some enticing opportunities.

Mesrine fashioned a rough knife out of the handle of an aluminium mug, sharpening it on a wall. On 17 August 1969, a guard was overpowered and locked in a cell. As only three warders were on duty during the evening shift, Mesrine had no difficulty in wandering round the jail until he found Jeanne Schneider. The couple even had time to steal food from the kitchens before escaping through the exercise yard.

It was outside the prison that they encountered real problems. The single feasible route lay through thick forests and, in the rain, they made slow progress. In the morning, a search party with tracker dogs hunted them down. Soon after, faced with overwhelming evidence, Mesrine and Schneider pleaded guilty to the kidnapping and were sentenced to ten and five years in jail respectively. The murder trial, which began on 18 January 1971, was more controversial. Defence lawyers were able to show inconsistencies in the evidence of some of the dead

woman's relations. As a result of these witnesses' over-zealous attempts to incriminate Mesrine, he and Jeanne were acquitted, although the judge was clearly unhappy at this verdict.

Mesrine was taken back to the top-security wing of the St Vincent-de-Paul gaol in Laval to serve his sentence for the kidnapping. This was the showpiece of the Canadian prison system. It had been specially constructed in 1968, at a cost of 2.5 million dollars, to house inveterate would-be escapers. In the correctional unit, there were 65 warders guarding 62 prisoners. The place was reckoned to be escape-proof.

> **“Money, power and social position . . . these are nothing less than other forms of terrorism”**
>
> JACQUES MESRINE

On 21 August 1972, Mesrine and four other men broke out of the prison during an exercise period. One was swiftly recaptured, but the others reached the nearby Highway 25, where they flagged down two passing cars and completed their getaway. The escape, which exposed the incompetence of the prison system, became front-page news.

Mesrine returned to Montreal, where he joined forces with Jean-Paul Mercier, another of the escapees. The two men had much in common. Although eight years younger than Mesrine, Mercier was a hardened criminal who had been serving 24 years for attempted murder and kidnapping. Like Mesrine, he already had one previous jail break to his credit.

High-speed risks

Only one week after the break-out, on 28 August, the two men robbed the Toronto Dominion Bank in Montreal, before embarking on a reckless scheme that carried Mesrine's signature. His stay in the correctional unit at Laval had fired his resentment at purpose-built, high-security blocks. He was determined to return to Laval and spring the remaining inmates from the correctional unit.

However, as Mesrine, Mercier and Mercier's girlfriend, Suzanne Francoeur, approached the jail, they saw that extra guards had been stationed both inside and outside the walls. Despite this, Mesrine opened fire on a nearby police car. Shots were returned and the two criminals fled ignominiously. This pointless act of bravado offered a tragic foretaste of the deadly crime to come.

On 3 September 1972, the three spent a pleasant afternoon in the large wooded area to the north of the city. They managed to find a remote spot, where they expected to be un-

Rex Features

BACKGROUND

BLONDE BEAUTY

Jocelyne Deraiche came from a large, French-speaking family, living in a respectable suburb of Montreal. At 19, she was seventeen years younger then Mesrine, whom she met at a party outside Montreal after his escape from prison. She was entranced by the glamorous lifestyle which Mesrine appeared to lead and accompanied him out of her homeland to the United States, Venezuela, and then France. Eventually, however, the disadvantages of staying with a wanted criminal became apparent. Jocelyne's Canadian accent was very conspicuous in France, forcing her to keep a low profile, and she soon became homesick. Nor did Jocelyne's problems end after her return to Canada. She was sentenced to 23 months in prison for her part in helping Mercier escape and, when she travelled to France in 1978 to visit Mesrine in jail, she was arrested and tried for the earlier offence of using forged identity papers.

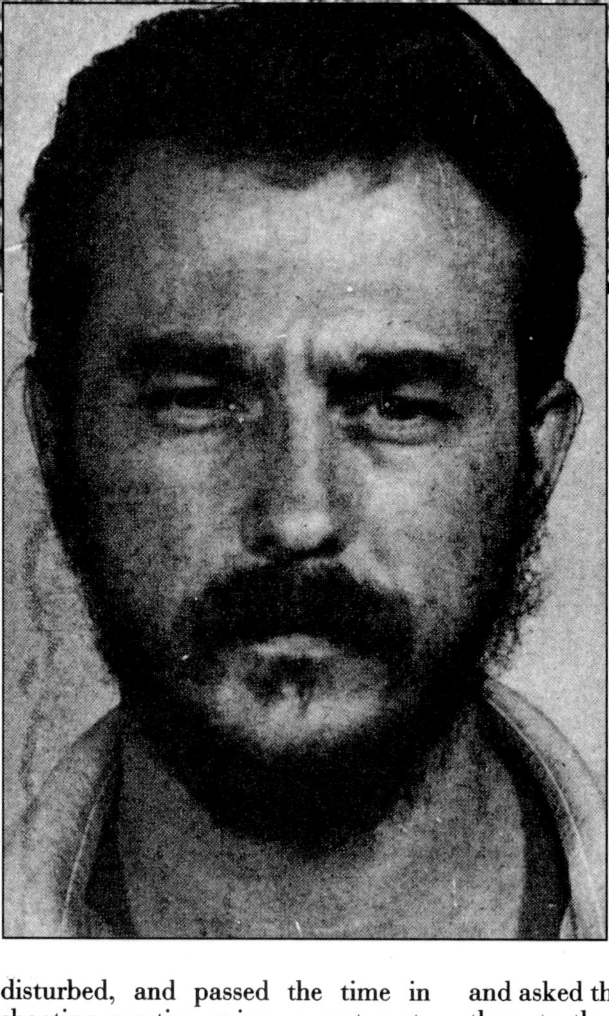

ALLO Police

In the daring escape from St Vincent-de-Paul prison (above), Mesrine provided the inspiration for inmates such as André Ouellette (left) and Michel Lafleur (right) to find a way across barriers which would have defeated them on their own. Mesrine's mind worked at high speed and with great ingenuity during these escapades.

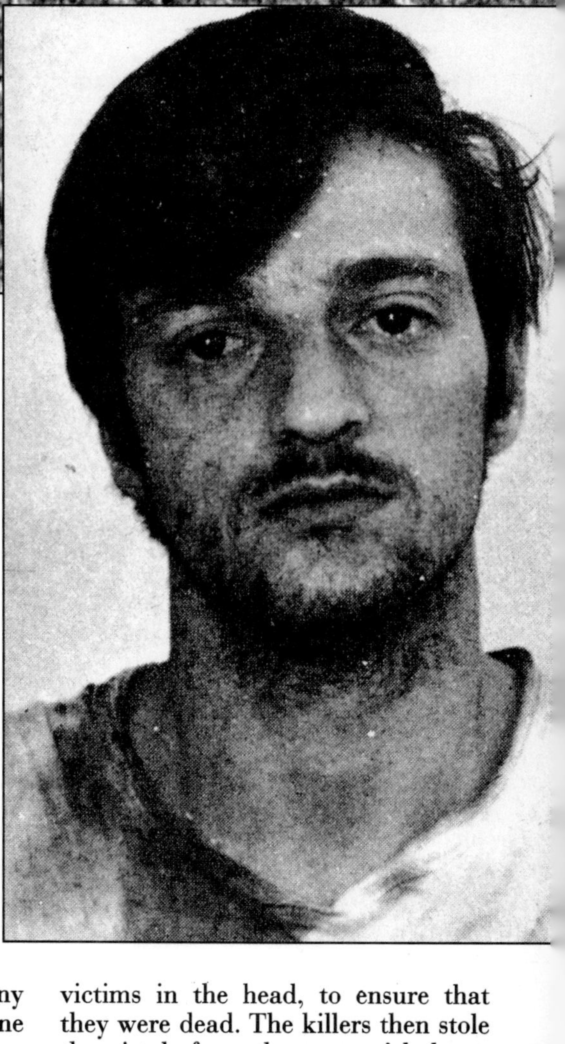

disturbed, and passed the time in shooting practice, using paper targets pinned to the trees.

Late in the afternoon, on their way home, they were stopped for a routine check by two forest rangers, Mederic Côté and Ernest Saint-Pierre. Opening the boot of the car, the rangers were astonished to find an assortment of at least 12 loaded guns and asked the strangers to accompany them to the warden's office. Mesrine and Mercier refused.

Double murder

It was at this moment that the two rangers realized they had chanced upon serious villains. An instant later they had been gunned down. As they lay on the ground, Mesrine shot both victims in the head, to ensure that they were dead. The killers then stole the pistols from the rangers' holsters and a rifle from their pick-up truck. They covered the two bodies with leaves and left them on a nearby dirt track, where they were discovered two days later. They had been middle-aged men, used to dealing only with the occasional poacher.

Mesrine, Mercier and Suzanne drove back to Montreal but, despite the public outrage about the deaths of the forest rangers, did not leave the city immediately. Mesrine smuggled a message to Jeanne Schneider, offering to help her escape. But Jeanne had heard that police were circulating the names of Mesrine and Mercier as suspects in the forest killings, and chose to serve out her sentence.

A journey south

The two men did not lie in hiding for long. A few days after the shootings, they robbed a bank opposite their apartment.

Three days later, they robbed it again. This was exhibitionism by Mesrine, who had seen a cashier looking disgusted as they left the building after the first raid. On the second, it was she who was ordered to empty the tills. Mesrine warned her not to scowl as they left the bank or they would rob it a third time. He had felt slighted at being held in disdain by a minor employee of a bank over which he was demonstrating his superiority.

Finally, Mesrine and Mercier decided to drive south into the United States and, from there, to travel to South America.

They did not travel alone. Mercier was accompanied by Suzanne and Mesrine by his new 19 year-old mistress, Jocelyne Deraiche. She had met Jacques while he was masquerading under the alias of Bruno Dansereau, and soon she fell under the spell of his charm.

The foursome crossed the border and headed for New York. They remained there briefly while Mesrine made arrangements for them to settle in Venezuela. The OAS network helped him to procure the false papers he needed to establish a new identity.

New frontiers

In Venezuela, the group moved into a luxurious villa near Caracas. Mesrine and Mercier intended to 'commute' periodically into the United States to continue their bank raids. However, Suzanne required an operation and Mercier accompanied her back to Canada. Then, soon after, Mesrine learned that Interpol were on his trail and that he might not be safe in Venezuela. He was running out of places to hide, and so decided on a typically bold course of action. At some time in December 1972, Mesrine and Jocelyne flew to Spain, hired a car and quietly drove across the border into France.

ALLO Police

The most evil accomplice Mesrine ever found was Jean-Paul Mercier (above), a heartless killer. Together they committed a double murder.

DEATH IN THE WILDS

THE VICTIMS

ALLO Police

Mederic Côté, 62, had been a forest ranger for 23 years and lived in the nearby town of Plessisville. He is believed to have been the first to have recognised the prisoners, and was shot in the chest by Mesrine.

GIP

Ernest Saint-pierre, 52, another French-Canadian, lived in St Louis de Blandford with a young family and had been a forest ranger for 12 years. He was shot in the stomach by Mercier.

THE DEADLY OAS

Mesrine was taught his skills by a fanatical right-wing force that used murder and bombing against the helpless.

Popperfoto

Violent political riots erupted in Algeria during the late 1950s as French troops fought young nationalists (above). Mesrine came to dislike Arabs, and enjoyed operations against them. He later joined the OAS (Organisation de l'Armée Secrète), the private army formed by General Salan (ringed, in centre). After retiring as head of the French forces in Algeria, Salan's loyalties changed and he determined to block French moves to decolonize Algeria.

Popperfoto

French paratroopers hold back an enthusiastic crowd (above) during the visit of President de Gaulle of France to Constantine, Algeria, in June 1958. But the sinister OAS produced posters of de Gaulle and his supporters (right), which declared, 'The OAS strikes where it likes, when it likes, any way it likes.' Its methods usually ended in street shoot-outs (below), explosions and the deaths of many innocent people. The training that Mesrine received from the OAS stood him in good stead many times during his criminal activities.

ALGÉROISES,
ALGÉROIS !

REGARDEZ CES TRAITRES

QUE LEUR IMAGE RESTE EN VOS MEMOIRES, LE SYMBOLE DE LA DECHEANCE DE LA DICTATURE GAULLISTE ET L'INSULTE DU POUVOIR A TOUS CEUX QUI SONT MORTS POUR NOTRE PATRIE
L'O.A.S. A DEJA PUNI CERTAINS, LES AUTRES SERONT BIENTOT CHATIES SANS PITIE

Le chef et quelques-uns de ses barbouzes

BUI THE Roger
EXECUTE
RENOIST Robert
EXECUTE
SON-TAY
EXECUTE
VILLONGA

TRANG TRONG
VEILLARD
SARRADY Nasser
TOUITOU Joseph

L'OAS frappe où elle veut, quand elle veut, comme elle veut

Rex Features; above: Popperfoto

THREE

THE HUNT

Chased In Paris

The French net was slowly tightening around Mesrine. But he had learnt how to laugh, even in defeat, and from prison he spun legends and fancies which fed a country's hunger for anarchic heroes.

KEY DATES

MAR 73-MAY 77

5.3.73	Mesrine shoots police officer in Paris bar
8.3.73	Police arrest Mesrine
6.6.73	Mesrine escapes from courthouse in Compiègne
27.9.73	Mesrine surrenders to 'anti-gangs' unit
14.5.77	Sentenced to 20 years' imprisonment for robbery and shooting

Mesrine's stealthy return to Paris, after nearly five years on the American continent, was like a homecoming. Undaunted at being an international fugitive, he delighted in showing Jocelyne the sights, buying her new clothes and dining with her in the finest Parisian restaurants.

At the same time, he was keen to re-establish his old lifestyle as soon as possible. This meant finding new hideouts and stocking them with furniture, clothes and an array of guns. Whenever possible, Mesrine preferred

A telephoto lens captures Mesrine (above) inside the top-security prison in Paris after his arrest in 1973. He already had plans to escape. His arsenal (right) included eight automatic weapons, eight machine guns, four shotguns and three rifles.

Syndication International

to keep several bases, in case one hideout had to be abandoned at very short notice. This was expensive and Mesrine soon resumed a routine of armed robberies and hold-ups.

But things had changed during his absence. Mesrine was now a much bigger fish. Interpol was on his trail and his prolific activity – Mesrine committed more than a dozen crimes in the first two months of 1973 – meant that capture was inevitable.

On 5 March, Mesrine entered the 'Dixie' bar, near the Place de la Madeleine. During the course of a quarrel, Mesrine smashed bottles behind the bar and menaced customers with a Colt .45 pistol. A policeman tried to intervene and Mesrine fired, wounding the officer, whose two shots in return hit a door-frame.

Mesrine made good his escape by hijacking a taxi. But the police had already located his hideout by tailing a known accomplice from one of his bank jobs. Mesrine was staying at a flat that he had rented from a judge – the sort of comic gesture which he appreciated – and detectives kept careful watch on this for several days. On 8 March, they surprised Mesrine in the hallway as he returned from the shops. The operation was bloodless

Rex Features

Sygma

By his return from Canada, Mesrine (above) was equipped like a one-man private army. 'You know I wouldn't hurt a fly,' he teased one senior police officer.

and efficient.

Mesrine's arrest was followed by a flowering in his public reputation. At his flat at 1, Rue Pierre Grenier, the police had uncovered a treasure trove of cash, travellers' cheques, false passports and firearms. Their astonishment mounted when, during his interrogation, Mesrine claimed to have committed 39 murders.

As soon as they started to investigate these 'killings', the police became sceptical. However, news of this boast filtered through to the press and, immediately, the name Mesrine was in the headlines. A myth was born. Mesrine wasted no time in con-

solidating the legend. As he was led off to La Santé prison to await trial, he turned to a policeman and asked: 'What do you bet me that I'll be free within 3 months?'

Mesrine had already completed checks on the courthouse in Compiègne, where he knew he would appear if ever arrested. On 6 June 1973, he was taken there to face a minor charge of passing dud cheques six years before. An accomplice had smuggled a Luger pistol into the lawyers' toilet. Mesrine retrieved it and took the magistrate hostage. The unfortunate man was dragged out into the courtyard, where a friend of Mesrine was waiting in an Alfa Romeo. Releasing his hostage, Mesrine sprinted to the car amid a hail of bullets. He was wounded in the arm, but his driver had been well briefed and got them to the isolated farmhouse chosen as their refuge.

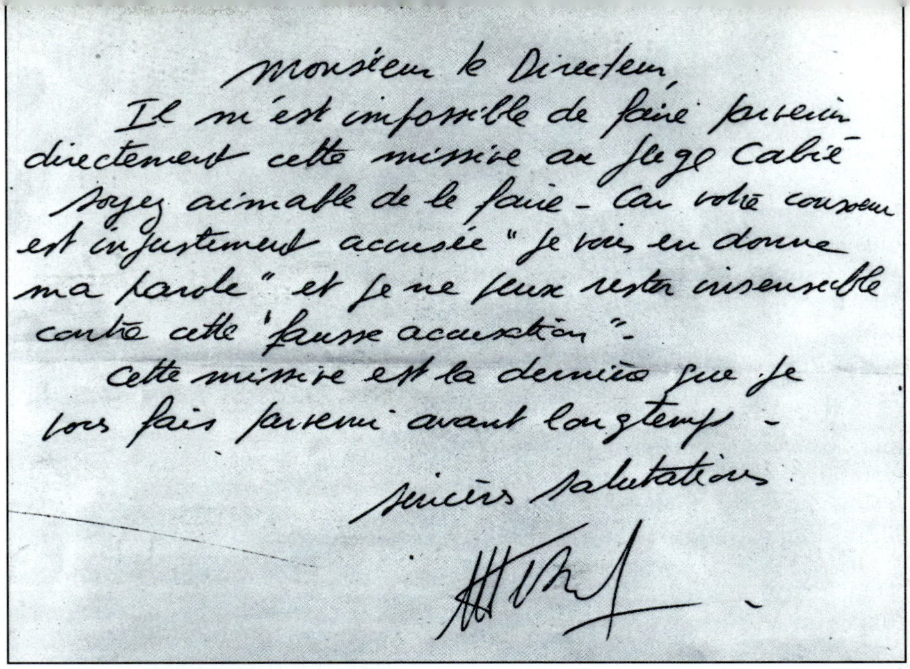
Monsieur le Directeur,
Il m'est impossible de faire parvenir directement cette missive au Juge Cabié soyez aimable de le faire – car votre cousine est injustement accusée "je vous en donne ma parole" et je ne peux rester insensible contre cette 'fausse accusation'.
Cette missive est la dernière que je vous fais parvenir avant longtemps –
sincères salutations

Popperfoto

Always courting publicity, Mesrine wrote several letters to the police while he was in prison, complaining that he had been falsely accused.

Within a fortnight, Jocelyne had joined Mesrine and they moved into a flat in the seaside resort of Trouville. In a typical show of bravado, Mesrine selected an apartment that was only yards away from police headquarters and then rapidly befriended one of the local officers. His elaborate disguise made him virtually unrecognizable in short hair, a thick beard and the kind of casual clothes that ran counter to the debonair image presented of him in the press.

Mesrine enjoyed the summer, visiting the nearby racecourse and casinos, until Jocelyne flew back to Canada in September. Mesrine had by this time been returning to Paris to commit further robberies. He had developed the tactic of executing these in tandem, moving on directly from his initial hold-up to carry out a second.

On 27 September 1973, during one of these double robberies, the registration number of the getaway car was spotted as Mesrine and his accomplices were leaving a bank and the police located it while the second robbery was in progress. Mesrine escaped, but one of his men was wounded and the inexperienced driver, Pierre Verheyden, was arrested. He soon gave detectives a number of important clues.

Verheyden's information led police to Mesrine's hideout in the Rue Vergniaud. The specialist 'anti-gangs' unit, with its team of sharpshooters, was called out and the apartment was sealed off. The officer in charge, Commissaire Robert Broussard, ordered his men to move in. He called out to Mesrine to give himself up. Realizing that he was surrounded, Mesrine agreed after stalling for just long enough to burn some of the more incriminating evidence within his flat. Inside, he had laid out his armoury of guns and ammunition like a soldier's kit awaiting the inspection of a commanding officer.

The theatrical surrender was clearly

> **I am not a public enemy. I am an enemy of a public service, the banks. I have eaten the cake, not the grandmother or the Little Red Riding Hood**
>
> MESRINE at his trial, May 1977

IN CONTEXT

THE ANTI-GANGS

In the public eye, Commissaire Robert Broussard (below) came to be seen as the arch-antagonist of Mesrine in a thrilling battle of wits. It was, inevitably, Mesrine who was promoting this idea. Broussard was a high-profile officer, celebrated for his success in smashing a Marseilles drug ring and for his dealings with Palestinian terrorists. His Brigade de Recherche et d'Intervention (popularly called the 'anti-gangs') was the crack unit of the Paris Prefecture, but it had a reputation for being trigger happy. Mesrine kept his own album of press cuttings about notable police officers and was flattered that it was Broussard who led the siege of his apartment. After opening the door to surrender, Mesrine poured champagne. Broussard accepted the drink and suffered no ill effects.

Popperfoto

Rex Features

to the stage after a long absence. He played his part well, and the press and the public hung on his every word.

Applause in court

Newspaper correspondents noted how he had the cheerful, confident air of a military commander. Mesrine winked at journalists and flirted with a female lawyer. When the list of his false passports and identity papers was read out in court, Mesrine turned to Judge Charles Petit and told him that by the following morning he could have one made out in his name. His moment of triumph came when he removed, from the knot of his tie, a tiny plaster impression of the keys to his handcuffs, which he had bought from a guard. Joyfully, Mesrine threw the plaster cast into the crowd and the gallery erupted. The judge was less amused. Mesrine was sentenced to 20 years' imprisonment. But he was not too disheartened. He had decided not to serve the full term.

Mesrine's lawyers (above) seem infected by his humour at his trial in May 1977, but the judge, Charles Petit (right), was to become a target of revenge.

Rex Features

designed to attract attention. Soon, stories about Mesrine monopolized the headlines. Many were highly fanciful and Mesrine tried to bring lawsuits against four papers for defamation of character. But it was to be three-and-a-half years before he stood inside a courtroom again.

Rich imagination

During the long wait, Mesrine wrote an autobiography in which he portrayed himself as a brutal, vengeful killer. Its contents were recognized as pure invention and the book was seen as a glorified press release.

Mesrine made other attempts to maintain public interest. In November 1975, he smuggled out a letter containing a death threat against a journalist named Jacques Derogy, who had written an article critical of the prisoner. At the same time, Mesrine developed his case for prison reform. He saw no contradiction in being both homicidal and philanthropic.

Overall, time weighed heavily on Mesrine. When, on 3 May 1977, his trial finally opened, he felt like a great actor making a triumphant comeback

IN CONTEXT

TALL STORY

Throughout his career, Mesrine was obsessed with his public image and loved to talk at length about his crimes. Ideally, he preferred to do this directly, through clandestine interviews with the press. However, during his long confinement in La Santé prison in Paris, he decided to write his autobiography. The manuscript was smuggled out of prison and, after a long search for a publisher, it eventually reached the shops in February 1977 under the title of *'L'Instinct de Mort'* (The Killing Instinct). In the book, Mesrine adopted the persona of a brutal murderer who slays his victims without mercy or remorse. As usual, his claims were wildly exaggerated – one newspaper described the book as a novel disguised as autobiography – and the police were never able to substantiate any of the graphically described 'murders'. Even so, the authorities were appalled at this blatant piece of exploitation and eventually passed a ruling, popularly known as 'Mesrine's law', which barred any criminal from making a profit out of his offences. Mesrine threatened to write another book entitled 'Guilty of being Innocent'.

TALKING POINT

VERSIONS OF JUSTICE

The French and British legal systems differ in crucial ways. Each has its strengths and weaknesses.

The long wait of over 3½ years between Mesrine's arrest and the start of his final trial highlights one of the differences between the French and British legal systems. In France, criminal proceedings against a suspect are conducted in three main stages. A preliminary enquiry is carried out by the police. This is followed by the *'instruction préparatoire'*, during which the detainee is brought before an examining magistrate and questioned. Finally, there is the *'instruction définitive'*, the trial itself.

The crucial distinction

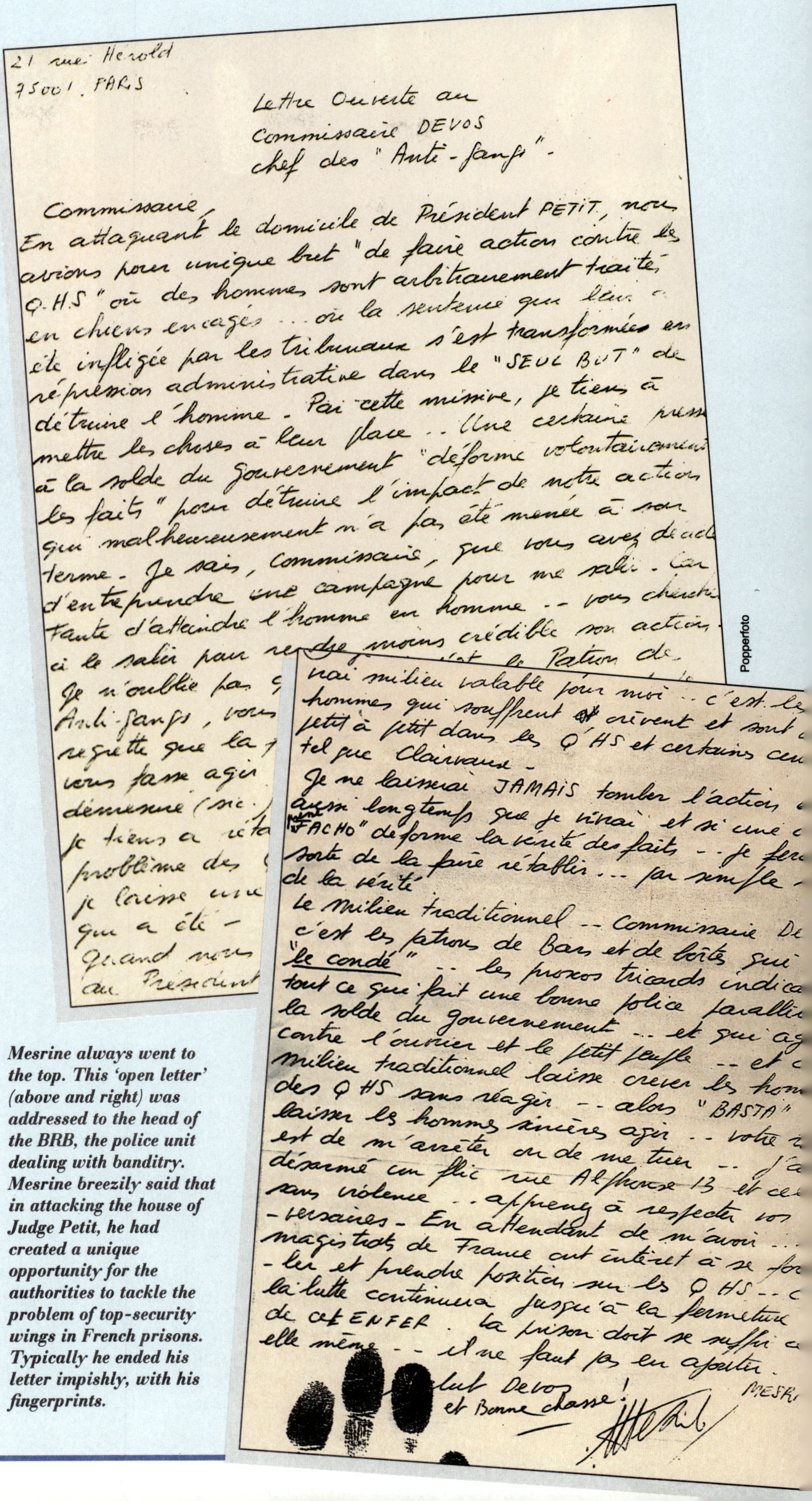
21 rue Herold
75001. PARIS

Lettre Ouverte au
Commissaire DEVOS
chef des "Anti-gangs".

Commissaire,
En attaquant le domicile de Président PETIT, nous
avions pour unique but "de faire action contre les
Q.H.S" où des hommes sont arbitrairement traités
en chiens encagés ... où la sentence qui leur a
été infligée par les tribunaux s'est transformée en
répression administrative dans le "SEUL BUT" de
détruire l'homme. Par cette missive, je tiens à
mettre les choses à leur place.. Une certaine presse
à la solde du Gouvernement "déforme volontairement
les faits" pour détruire l'impact de notre action
qui malheureusement n'a pas été menée à son
terme. Je sais, Commissaire, que vous avez décidé
d'entreprendre une campagne pour me salir. Car
faute d'atteindre l'homme en homme -- vous cherchez
à le salir pour rendre moins crédible son action.
... le Patron de
Je n'oublie pas q
Anti-gangs, vous
regrette que la
vous fasse agir
démesure (sic.)
je tiens à réta
problème des
je laisse une
qui a été -
Quand nous
au Président

vrai milieu valable pour moi -- c'est les
hommes qui souffrent et crèvent et sont
petit à petit dans les Q HS et certains ce
tel que Clairvaux.
Je ne laisserai JAMAIS tomber l'action
aussi longtemps que je vivrai et si une
"FACHO" déforme la vérité des faits -- je fer
sorte de la faire rétablir... par simple
de la vérité.
Le Milieu traditionnel -- Commissaire De
c'est les patrons de Bars et de boîtes qui
"le condé" -- les proxos tricards indica
tout ce qui fait une bonne police parallè
la solde du Gouvernement -- et qui ag
contre l'ouvrier et le petit peuple -- et
milieu traditionnel laisse crever les hom
des Q HS sans réagir -- alors "BASTA"
laisser les hommes sincères agir -- votre
est de m'arrêter ou de me tuer -- j'a
désarmé un flic rue Alphonse 13 et ce
sans violence.. apprenez à respecter vos
-versaires- En attendant de m'avoir ...
magistrats de France ont intérêt à se fo
-ler et prendre position sur les Q HS -- c
la lutte continuera jusqu'à la fermeture
de ces ENFER. La prison doit se suffire à
elle même -- il ne faut pas en ajouter.
Salut Devos
et Bonne chasse!
MESRI

Popperfoto

Mesrine always went to the top. This 'open letter' (above and right) was addressed to the head of the BRB, the police unit dealing with banditry. Mesrine breezily said that in attacking the house of Judge Petit, he had created a unique opportunity for the authorities to tackle the problem of top-security wings in French prisons. Typically he ended his letter impishly, with his fingerprints.

lies in the second stage, where the *'juge d'instruction'* (examining magistrate) plays a greater part than his English counterpart. It is his job to determine whether or not there is sufficient evidence to bring a case to trial. In so doing, the examining magistrate controls the direction of the investigation. His powers allow him to arrest, to order searches and to seize private property. In addition, he can summon and interrogate witnesses, demand forensic tests and even arrange for reconstructions of the crime to be staged. In theory, a French examining magistrate will devote as much energy to seeking evidence of a suspect's innocence as of his guilt.

Scales of justice

The French and British systems of justice were not always so different, however. In Britain until the 19th century, justices of the peace used to interrogate suspects in much the same way as a French examining magistrate does now. This changed when the granting of a prisoner's right to remain silent undermined the inquisitorial process and the role of inquiry was assumed by the rapidly developing police force. French judicial procedure, however, does not recognize the same right of silence.

In contrast, when a defendant is charged, an English magistrate's function is to consider the police evidence and, where necessary, to commit the accused for trial at the Crown Court. The magistrate takes no part in the investigation. As a result, the tone of a French investigation is classified as 'inquisitorial', as opposed to the 'adversarial' system in Britain.

Hint of guilt

In Britain, the impartial weighing-up of evidence takes place during a trial, when the onus is on the prosecution to prove the accused's guilt. In France, this assessment has occurred at an earlier point and the very fact that the case has come to trial is sometimes taken as an indication of a defendant's guilt. The criminal record of the accused is not excluded from court and the defence counsel's rights of cross-examination are restricted. As a result, the conviction rate for serious crime is much higher in France than it is in Britain.

Advocates of the French system argue that this has a number of advantages. It is said that the early involvement of the judiciary greatly reduces the possibility of police malpractice and that it filters out many of the more trivial cases that come to court in Britain.

Against this is the problem of remand. In France, a person can be held throughout the investigations and these detainees form a far higher percentage of the prison population than in Britain. At its worst, this can produce severe miscarriages of justice. Marie Besnard, for example, was suspected of poisoning members of her family and the police investigations lasted for 12 years before she was finally acquitted in 1961.

A notorious case

A law was passed in 1970 to reduce such prolonged detentions, but there is still the notorious case of Simone Weber, who has been held on remand in a prison in the town of Nancy for more than four years, still uncertain if she is to be tried for the murder of her ex-lover.

Rex Features

Marie Besnard (above) signs copies of her memoirs after enduring a 12-year wait to be acquitted.

Simone Weber's ordeal (below) – four years in prison without a trial – highlights a problem of the French legal system.

Syndicated Features

JUDGE PETIT

The French legal system formed part of the reason for Mesrine's vendetta against Judge Charles Petit, who had presided over the trial that ended with a 20-year sentence against the defendant. In France, a judge normally retires with a jury to consider the verdict, often making the outcome a personal matter between the judge and the accused. In Mesrine's case, the jury looked weary and strained when, after 13½ hours of deliberations, they returned to court. The judge is said to have pressed strongly for a longer sentence.

Mesrine's feud with the judge was also motivated by his campaign for prison reform. He saw judges as being accomplices of the faults of the penal system and demanded that they be made to visit prisons before sentencing people. When he finally carried out his plot against the judge, Mesrine harangued the Petit family about the destructive effects of top-security wings.

FOUR

THE KIDNAPS

Closing In

Mesrine had decided he was too big for any prison and too grand to be recaptured. Deep down, he knew the end was close. But there was still time to settle a feud with a man who had belittled him.

Sygma

La Santé, the prison in Paris where Mesrine was confined, had the reputation of being escape-proof. No one had ever broken out of it. A new top-security wing had been built and this became Mesrine's home.

On the morning of 8 May 1978, Mesrine was led into an interview room in his wing for a routine meeting with Christiane Giletti, one of his lawyers. The guard was sent away to fetch some papers. In his absence, Mesrine leapt up on a chair and removed the cover from a ventilation duct. Concealed there were pistols, tear gas pellets, a knife and a length of blue moutaineering rope.

Outside, an accomplice, François Besse, had overpowered a guard and, with a third prisoner, burst into the nearby staff office. The warders there were relieved of their guns, papers and keys, and the three convicts swiftly changed into the navy blue uniforms of the prison guards.

In the courtyard, the bogus warders instructed some workmen to move their ladders to the outer wall of the prison. Ten days before the escape, Mesrine had spotted these builders fitting new grilles on to cell windows and had altered his plans to make use of their presence.

It was only when they saw 'warders' climbing up the outer wall with mountaineering gear that the perimeter guards realised something was amiss. Shots rang out. The third prisoner was killed, but Mesrine and

Police seal off the streets outside the top-security La Santé prison in Paris (above) after Mesrine and another prisoner had escaped over the wall on 8 May 1978. Mesrine fired back at security guards and appealed to a woman with a pram to take cover. The third and last man over, Carman Rives (right), was shot dead by the guards.

Besse got clear. Still wearing their official uniforms, they flagged down the driver of a white Renault, forced him out, and drove off to a flat near Les Invalides.

Back at La Santé, the air duct in the interview room was found to contain another gun, a hand grenade and a dagger. Mesrine's grappling iron was hidden behind bookshelves in an adjoining room. Clearly, there had been considerable assistance from outside.

The press had a field day, but the police hierarchy was deeply worried and even President Giscard d'Estaing made known his displeasure. An intensive manhunt was launched.

At 11 p.m. on 27 May 1978, Mesrine and Besse strode confidently into the police headquarters at the Normandy resort of Deauville and, introducing themselves as policemen, asked to see the Duty Inspector. On being told that he was out, the pair left quietly, promising to call again. Mesrine judged that there would be few officers around at that time and that he and Besse would be able to seize some uniforms and guns.

From the police station, the two men walked directly to the casino. There, they used Ministry of Justice identity cards, which they had stolen during their escape from La Santé, to gain access to the Cashier's Office, where they demanded money at gunpoint. But someone sounded an alarm and, when Mesrine and Besse emerged from the casino, the police were waiting. The robbers tried to shoot their way out. Both men were wounded, Besse seriously. Two bystanders were also hit. Somehow, the gunmen managed to get away.

> **“I know it will end badly . . . the folklore and the champagne are finished. From now on, there's nothing left except war”**
>
> JACQUES MESRINE

On the run

During a desperate chase through the Normandy countryside, their first getaway car broke down. They stole another. More shots were exchanged as they drove through a police roadblock. The second car, damaged by gunfire, veered off into a ditch. Mesrine and Besse staggered across the fields and sheltered under trees while police helicopters circled overhead. They took hostages at an isolated farmhouse, forcing their captives to drive them towards Paris. Finally, they completed their journey in a rowing boat and in yet another stolen car.

Mesrine was undeterred by the nar-

Popperfoto

KEY DATES

MAY 78 - SEP 79

8.5.78	Mesrine escapes from La Santé prison
27.5.78	Shoot-out in Normandy
10.11.78	Bungled kidnapping of Judge Petit
21.6.79	Kidnapping of Henri Lelièvre
9.79	Mesrine returns to Paris after foreign trip

row escape and began planning his next crime. To attack a casino, he argued, was to attack the empire of vice. The only way to win against its bank was to use a gun. Similarly, Mesrine explained away his next big raid, on the Le Raincy branch of the Société Générale, as revenge. The Société Générale had been awarded substantial damages out of the earnings Mesrine had made from his book. At that time, Mesrine wrote angrily to its Director, accusing him of stealing his money and warning him to consider it only as a temporary loan.

Mesrine carried out the robbery while Besse held hostage the wife of a senior bank employee. Mesrine was tempted into trying his hand at kidnapping once more.

His victim was Judge Charles Petit, the man who had sentenced him to 20 years in jail. Mesrine planned to use the abduction of a prominent legal figure as a platform for airing his views on prison reform and the maximum security wings.

Besse wanted nothing to do with the scheme and Mesrine had to enlist the help of two raw recruits. Their inexperience proved crucial when the attack took place on 10 November

BACKGROUND

FATED COMPANIONS

The intoxicating excitement of Mesrine's company proved short-lived for most of his friends and accomplices. Jean-Paul Mercier, the killer of one of the Canadian forest rangers, was captured on 2 December 1972 and eventually sentenced to life imprisonment and a further 270 years. Mercier escaped on 22 October 1974 but was shot dead during a bank raid in Montreal eight days later. His escape had been conceived in Paris by Mesrine, who wanted Mercier to help him escape in due course, and assisted by Jocelyne Deraiche, who was sentenced to 23 months in jail. After her release, she was arrested in France and charged with using false identity papers. She was tried in 1978, given a nominal prison sentence, which she had already served on remand, and deported.

BACKGROUND

CAREER ASSESSMENT

The abduction of Henri Lelièvre (below) was Mesrine's last ambitious crime. He was increasingly attracted by kidnapping, partly because he thought it was safer. Being less 'public' than a bank hold-up, there was less risk of him being recognised. But he also needed one large haul to enable him to lie low. Life on the run was proving expensive and he was well aware that the police were fast closing in on him.

Lelièvre and Mesrine talked at length during the wait for the ransom, and the former acknowledged his captor's intelligence and thought that he might have made a successful businessman if he had chosen to pursue an honest career instead of choosing the path of crime.

Sygma; insets: Popperfoto

The 82 year-old Henri Lelièvre (left) was said to be among the 40 richest men in France. Mesrine kidnapped him at his home (above) with typical impudence. Police search the gang's hideout for clues (below).

1978. One of the judge's relations was able to alert the police and Mesrine was fortunate to escape unscathed. His next kidnapping venture was more carefully planned. Mesrine needed money and so the victim was a rich industrialist, Henri Lelièvre.

Once again, on 21 June 1979, Mesrine and his henchman posed as policemen, requesting their aged target to accompany them to the local station to help with some routine enquiries. Instead, they drove him to a rented house near Blois. Negotiations over the ransom were complex and lasted over a month. The police efficiently foiled the first delivery of the ransom, almost capturing Mesrine's accomplice in the process. After renewed threats, however, Lelièvre's son Michael made a clandestine payment, with the result that the elderly gentleman was released. Only then did the police find out that Mesrine had been behind the plot.

Time running out

The ransom of six million francs gave him precious breathing space. During the summer of 1979, he travelled to Italy and, perhaps, further afield to Algeria. Newspaper reports claimed that he also went to Spain or England. However, Mesrine knew his freedom was only a brief interlude. The banknotes from the Lelièvre kidnapping had been marked and, once laundered, would only be worth a percentage of their face value. Returning to Paris in the autumn of 1979, Mesrine faced having to resume his fraught and increasingly dangerous career as a bankrobber.

The pressure of living on the run was unremitting and Mesrine's mood was darkened by the knowledge that there could only be one way out. He would never go to jail again.

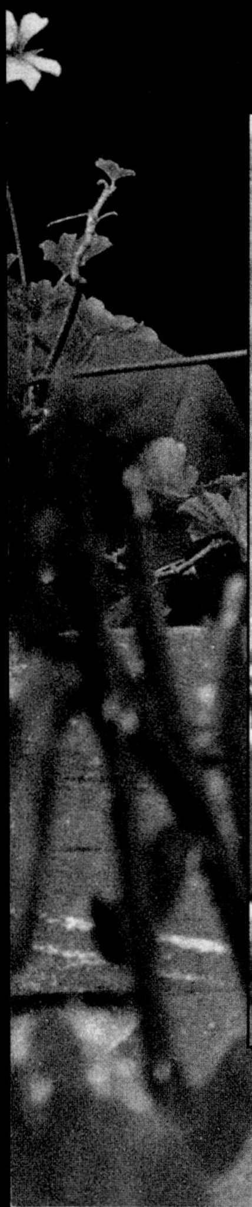

THEATRE OF DEATH

With his pride rocketing out of control, Mesrine turned to murder rather than submit to ordinary men.

Both: Sygma

After Mesrine's death, one newspaper described him as an unsavoury star who became the victim of his own inflated reputation. Certainly Mesrine had no desire to share the anonymity of most crooks, hiding away in some back-street dive to avoid being caught. He actively sought the limelight and, with his passionate interest in reading and collecting press-cuttings about himself, Mesrine was reminiscent of a temperamental actor fretting about his latest review.

Much of his criminal activity was motivated by a desire for attention. This may have been a legacy of the loneliness he felt when separated from his father during the war and, later, his boarding school years, or it may have been an attempt to recapture the praise he had won for his successful exploits in Algeria.

Party lover

Mesrine was naturally gregarious. All his favourite activities involved company – party-going, nightclubs, eating at fine restaurants, attending race meetings, gambling in casinos. They also required style. Mesrine was particular about the cut of his suit, the appearance of his women and the quality of his food and wine.

For his own security, he could not afford to trust or confide in many people. Yet he still possessed great personal warmth and magnetism. His prison guards and even the victims of his non-violent crimes remarked on his charm. From his friends, he commanded respect and unswerving loyalty.

Jacques' early grudge against figures of authority and his decision to concentrate his attacks on big institutions like the banks won him the unspoken admiration of many law-abiding citizens. Then, as his dramatic escapes made him more newsworthy, Mesrine's attempts to manipulate his own public image increased. There were theatrical gestures, such as offering champagne to the police. There were also defiant touches – introducing himself to his victims, lingering too long at the scene of a crime, walking into police stations – which courted disaster as well as column inches in the press.

Violent folly

Whatever his fantasies or secret following in France, the murder which Mesrine is

known to have committed was characterized only by its meanness and stupidity. The middle-aged forest ranger, Mederic Côté, was armed but could never have out-drawn Mesrine, and could easily have been disarmed and tied up with his partner while the attackers made their escape.

It is possible that Mesrine felt resentful and belittled by the fact that two mere forest rangers – not police officers, and not even French forest rangers – tried to detain him. He saw himself as writ large, and arrest by a forest ranger old enough to be his father would have destroyed his image of himself.

Deep loathing

The two shots he fired into the forest rangers' heads before concealing their bodies indicates some deep well of loathing inside Mesrine. He was to claim that he wanted to ensure that the men were dead. As a criminal, Mesrine was bold but, as a man, he lacked the bravery to confront his own fears and depressions.

Significantly, Mesrine felt no remorse for either forest ranger, only for the 12 year-old son of one of them, Ernest Saint-Pierre, crying by his father's grave. The photograph so disturbed Mesrine that he asked aloud if the boy knew his father had been allowed to kill in the name of the law. Only by thinking of the ranger as an agent of society could Mesrine deal with his distaste for himself.

This distaste may have motivated some of his later, grand fantasies in which Mesrine saw himself as a campaigner for prison reform, a Robin Hood figure and a doomed romantic hero, preferring death to mediocrity. No one knows if he ever looked within and saw the shallow cruelty of his true nature.

MESRINE AND THE PRESS

One of the most contentious issues raised by the Mesrine case was the role played by the press. Jacques had a flair for public relations and the news media were rarely slow to provide him with a platform. In addition to interviews, he often wrote open letters to the press, correcting factual errors in their reports of his crimes and airing his views on penal reform. In his final years, he also sent threatening letters to journalists who had written unflattering articles about him. To the police, the co-operation of the press bordered on collusion and they were particularly angry about interviews conducted in person with Mesrine, while he was on the run. The papers usually prefaced their stories by saying that, while they did not condone Mesrine's crimes, they believed their readers had a right to be informed.

Mesrine the gunman took a craftsman's pride in his arsenal (left). The Société Générale, Raincy (below), was the scene of one of the armed raids that made him notorious.

FIVE

THE END

Last Journey

Sygma

The French head of state believed Mesrine was undermining respect for law in the country. The finest police brains worked together to chase a man known for his daring and his ruthlessness with guns.

KEY DATES

10 AUG-2 NOV 79

10.8.79	Anti-Mesrine squad formed in Paris
10.9.79	Mesrine shoots Jacques Tillier in cave
24.10.79	Charly Bauer's car located
31.10.79	Mesrine's flat located
2.11.79	Mesrine shot dead by police

At the beginning of August 1979, the French authorities took a decisive initiative. A special anti-Mesrine squad was formed under the leadership of one of the most senior police officers in France, Commissaire Maurice Bouvier. He was to co-ordinate the efforts of the three serious crimes units, and thus try to eliminate all the rivalries that usually existed between these separate departments.

The three squads were the OCRB (Office Centrale de Repression de Banditisme) headed by Lucien Aimé-Blanc, the BRI (Brigade de Recherche et d'Intervention – the so-called 'anti-gangs') under Commissaire Broussard, and the BRB (Brigade de Repression de Banditisme), led by Serge Devos.

Within a month, the new unit had its first solid lead. On 10 September, a journalist named Jacques Tillier was found shot and wounded after a meeting with Mesrine in a cave, in the forest of Verneuil-en-Halatte. The latter even sent photographs of his victim to a Paris newspaper, explaining that he had punished the man for be-

traying him. This was a curious incident, as Mesrine was always keen to keep good relations with the press, and it seems likely that he believed Tillier to be a police informant.

In fact, Tillier did have police connections. In the past, he had been an inspector in the DST (Défense et Securité du Territoire), but his meeting with Mesrine had been arranged purely to write a story for his paper.

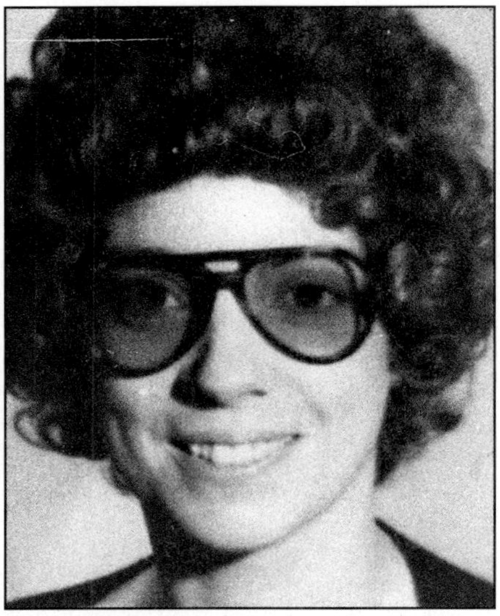

Sygma. Below: Rex FEatures

Detectives were less than pleased to find that, not for the first time, a reporter had withheld vital information from them.

As Tillier was questioned thoroughly by the police, one important clue emerged. Mesrine had an accomplice. From Tillier's memory, it was clear that this man had also been an inmate in one of the high-security blocks and this, combined with his physical description, eventually led them to the name of Charly Bauer.

It took detectives a further month to track Bauer down. Finally, on 24 October, they found his car parked in the St Lazare district of northern Paris. Bauer's girlfriend eventually collected the car and, from that moment, their flat in the Rue St Lazare was under constant surveillance.

Exactly one week later, Bauer led them to Rue Belliard, an address in the Montmartre area. The surveillance team watched intently as, moments later, Mesrine came out from the flats with his current mistress, Sylvie Jeanjacquot. Mesrine was disguised as an elderly man, walking with the aid of a stick, but the police were

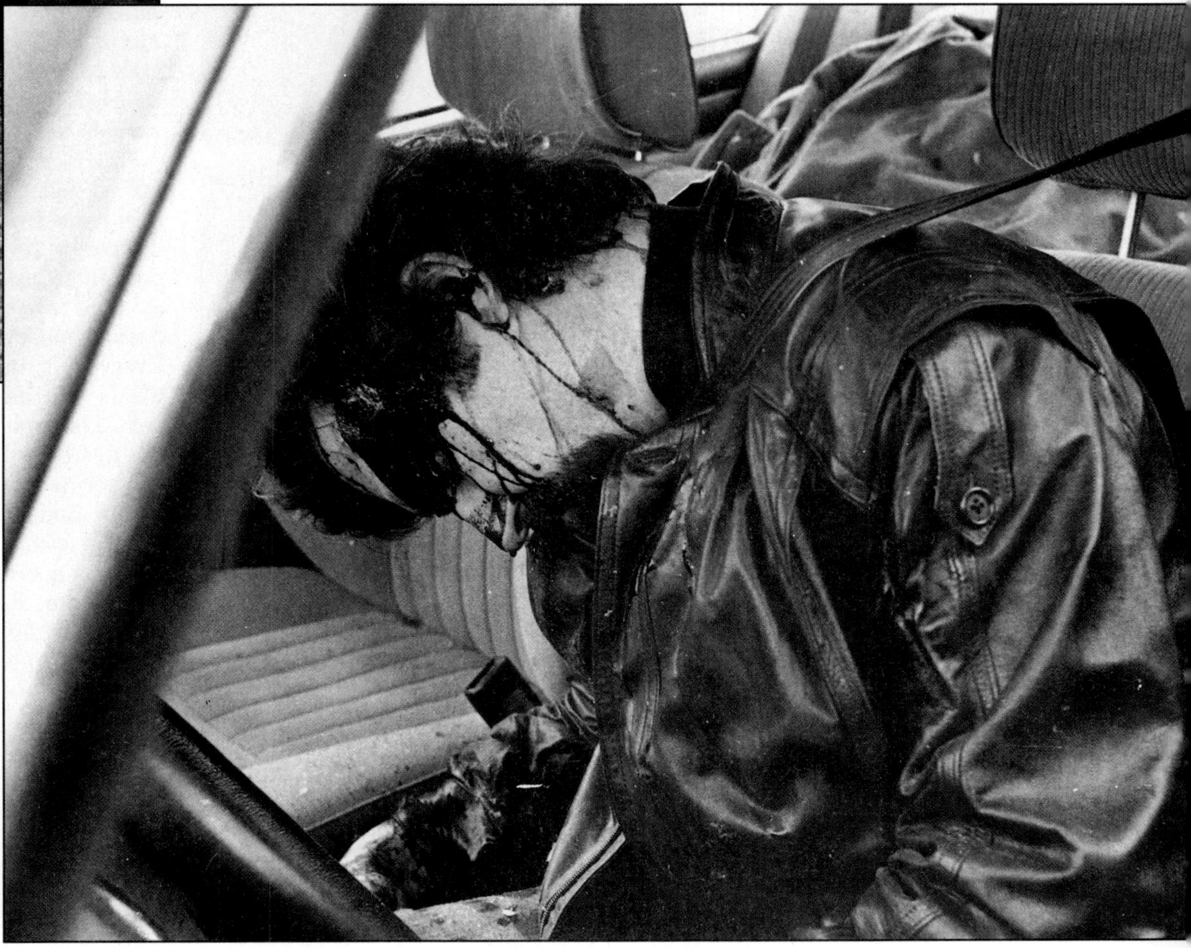

Commissaire Broussard (above, with beard) shares his relief that Mesrine's career is finally over. The sight of his body, riddled by 18 bullets (right) disturbs none of the team. The wig worn by Sylvie Jeanjacquot (above right) rests on the bonnet of the ambushed BMW after she was taken away, wounded in the deadly hail that had killed her lover.

convinced that they had found their quarry.

Eagerly they followed as Jacques and his friends went for a stroll up to the market in the Boulevard Ornano. There, they gazed at the window displays, paused to make some purchases at a furniture store and tried on some shoes in another shop, before returning to their base in the Rue Belliard.

The police were uncertain over how to approach Mesrine. They knew he would be armed. During his latest clandestine interview with the magazine *Paris Match*, he had deliberately allowed himself to be photographed with two revolvers stuffed into his belt. It was also known that he made a habit of carrying hand grenades.

Final vow

Moreover, Mesrine had repeatedly stressed his resolve never to be recaptured. 'The police must know that I'll never give in,' he had said in the interview. 'I won't go back to prison. I will shoot and it's too bad if innocent people get in the way. I won't shoot first, but I won't be the only corpse on the pavement.'

Much time and money had been invested in tracking Mesrine down. Many reputations were at stake. Now that he was cornered, it was imperative that no mistakes were made.

Accordingly, the building was staked out and a long wait began. Residents from the other flats were discreetly evacuated. Plain-clothes policemen and women masqueraded as road sweepers, gasmen, delivery boys, housewives and prostitutes. Everyone's nerves were on edge. A whole day passed and nobody came out. The police debated whether or not to storm the place.

Topham

A 25 year-old woman detective, Mireille Balestrazzi (left) masterminded the ambush with Commissaire Broussard (above). 'Did you think we would approach Mesrine with our police cards?', one officer asked.

Mesrine and Sylvie emerged just before 3 p.m. on Friday, 2 November. He was wearing a leather jacket and carrying a suitcase. She was clutching her white miniature poodle. They were going away for the weekend.

They climbed into a brown BMW saloon and set off. Soon, they turned into the Place de Clignancourt, near the Flea Market. A blue lorry, with a tarpaulin covering its load, signalled and cut across to turn right. Another lorry hemmed in the BMW from behind.

Suddenly, the tarpaulin on the blue lorry was thrown back, revealing a

CHARLY BAUER

IN CONTEXT

Mesrine's final accomplice was the unwitting instrument of his downfall. After interviewing Tillier, the police were sure that Bauer (right) was the second man involved in the attack and that he had assisted Mesrine in the Lelièvre kidnapping. The physical description fitted – mid-30s with a black moustache and a Marseilles accent – and, in common with Mesrine, he had come out with the same hotch-potch of left-wing theories that the police had come to associate with the maximum security wings. In fact, Bauer had served 16 years in Caen prison for drug trafficking.

Charly Bauer was tracked down and arrested at St Lazare on the day of Mesrine's death. Having already heard of his friend's fate, he offered no resistance, saying, 'The death of Le Grand (the great man) has broken me.'

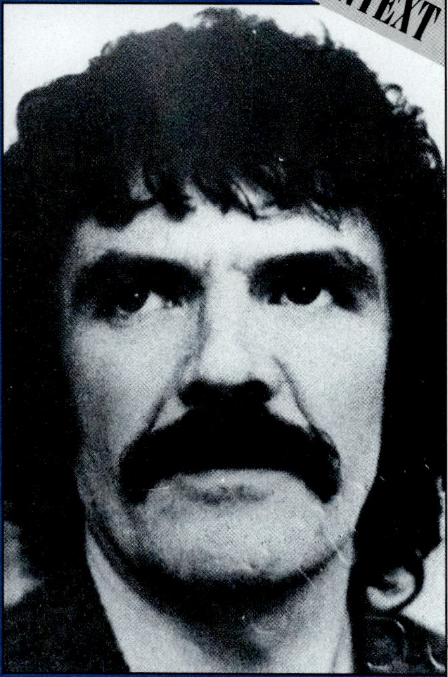

AGIP

Rex Features

IN CONTEXT

HIGH PLACES

The pursuit of Jacques Mesrine in the final months of his career was monitored carefully by President Giscard d'Estaing in the Elysée Palace. Every time the French cabinet met in the last half of 1979, the Interior Minister, Christian Bonnet, was asked, 'What have you got to report this week?' The Minister did not need to ask who the President of the Republic was referring to.

In the summer of that year, private guests of the President are reported to have enjoyed discussing Mesrine's exploits and to have described the French police as confused buffoons. Their host left the room, seething with dismay. A few days after this the anti-Mesrine squad was formed: Bonnet was told to find Mesrine or find another job.

Frank Spooner

Mesrine's funeral brought scores of people to the streets. One woman called him 'one of the last great anarchists'. Others simply remembered his charm.

group of police marksmen. Without warning, they opened fire and a salvo of high-velocity bullets tore through the windscreen. Mesrine was killed instantly. His body slumped forward over the steering wheel. One hand dangled down, towards the black bag at his feet, which contained his hand grenades. A car pulled up alongside the BMW. A man leaned out and fired one single shot into Mesrine's head.

Sylvie Jeanjacquot was severely wounded. She stumbled out of the passenger seat and took a few uncertain steps before collapsing on the cobblestones. An ambulance took her to the nearby Boucicault hospital, where her life was soon out of danger.

Into the streets

The small army of policemen and women involved in the operation surged forward from the surrounding streets. Swiftly, they cordoned off the area to hold back the gathering crowds. Their mood was one of jubilation, mingled with relief. Some officers embraced each other.

Mesrine's body remained in the car, sagging over his seat-belt for more than an hour. Nobody seemed to want to touch it. It was as if no one could believe that the hunt was finally over.

A crowd of 400 spectators built up around the barriers, jostling for a view. Mesrine's 18 year-old daughter Sabrina arrived and was led away in tears by a policeman. Finally, at 4.20 p.m., the police removed Mesrine's body. Broussard, his old adversary, helped to lift him from the car. A message was sent to the Paris Prefecture's headquarters: 'Mesrine has been killed. No casualties on our side.'

Detectives made a careful search of

MAURICE BOUVIER

The man chosen to co-ordinate the final manhunt for Mesrine was one of France's most celebrated policemen. Commissaire Bouvier (right) had dealt with crimes associated with the Algerian conflict. In two of the most notable operations, he had helped to break down OAS terrorist rings in France during the early 1960s and he was closely involved in foiling the assassination conspiracy against President de Gaulle in 1962. A quiet, pipe-smoking man, Bouvier provided the link between the different police squads engaged in the chase and their political leaders, who found Mesrine's freedom such an embarrassment.

Popperfoto. Above: Rex Features